THE LITTLE CITY OF HOPE

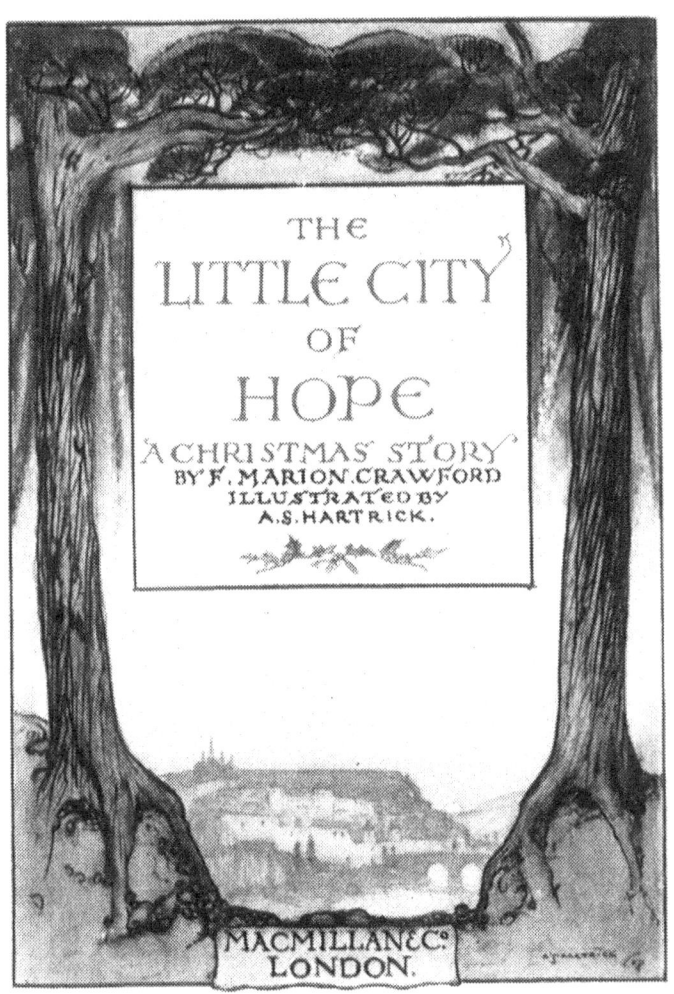

THE
LITTLE CITY
OF
HOPE
A CHRISTMAS STORY
BY F. MARION CRAWFORD
ILLUSTRATED BY
A.S. HARTRICK.

MACMILLAN & Co.
LONDON.

Wildside Press: 2003

Published by
Wildside Press, LLC
P.O. Box 301
Holicong, PA 18928-0301 USA
www.wildsidepress.com

Wildside Press Edition: MMIII

CONTENTS

ILLUSTRATIONS

THE LITTLE CITY OF HOPE

"HOPE IS VERY CHEAP. THERE'S ALWAYS PLENTY OF IT ABOUT."

I

HOW JOHN HENRY OVERHOLT SAT ON PANDORA'S BOX

"Hope is very cheap. There's always plenty of it about."

"Fortunately for poor men. Good morning."

With this mild retort and civil salutation John Henry Overholt rose and went towards the door, quite forgetting to shake hands with Mr. Burnside, though the latter made a motion to do so. Mr. Burnside always gave his hand in a friendly way, even when he had flatly refused to do what people had asked of him. It was cheap ; so he gave it.

But he was not pleased when they did not take it, for whatever he chose to give seemed of some value to him as soon as it was offered; even his hand. Therefore, when his visitor forgot to take it, out of pure absence of mind, he was offended, and spoke to him sharply before he had time to leave the private office.

"You need not go away like that, Mr. Overholt, without shaking hands."

The visitor stopped and turned back at once. He was thin and rather shabbily dressed. I know many poor men who are fat, and some who dress very well; but this was not that kind of poor man.

"Excuse me," he said mildly. "I didn't mean to be rude. I quite forgot."

He came back, and Mr. Burnside shook hands with becoming coldness, as having just given a lesson in manners. He was not a bad man, nor a miser, nor a Scrooge, but he was a great stickler for manners, especially with people who had nothing to give him. Besides, he had already lent Overholt money; or, to put it nicely, he had invested a little in his invention, and he did not see any reason why he should invest any more until it succeeded. Overholt called it selling shares, but Mr. Burnside called it borrowing money. Overholt was sure that if he could raise more

THE LITTLE CITY OF HOPE

funds, not much more, he could make a success of the " Air-Motor " ; Mr. Burnside was
equally sure that nothing would ever come of
it. They had been explaining their respective
points of view to each other, and in sheer
absence of mind Overholt had forgotten to
shake hands.

Mr. Burnside had no head for mechanics,
but Overholt had already made an invention
which was considered very successful, though
he had got little or nothing for it. The
mechanic who had helped him in its construction had stolen his principal idea before the
device was patented, and had taken out a
patent for a cheap little article which every
one at once used, and which made a fortune
for him. Overholt's instrument took its
place in every laboratory in the world ; but
the mechanic's labour-saving utensil took its
place in every house. It was on the strength
of the valuable tool of science that Mr. Burnside had invested two thousand dollars in the
Air-Motor without really having the smallest
idea whether it was to be a machine that
would move the air, or was to be moved by
it. A number of business men had done the
same thing.

3

THE LITTLE CITY OF HOPE

Then, at a political dinner in a club, three of the investors had dined at the same small table, and in an interval between the dull speeches, one of the three told the others that he had looked into the invention and that there was nothing in Overholt's Motor after all. Overholt was crazy.

" It's like this," he had said. " You know how a low-pressure engine acts ; the steam does a part of the work and the weight of the atmosphere does the rest. Now this man Overholt thinks he can make the atmosphere do both parts of the work with no steam at all, and as that's absurd, of course, he won't get any more of my money. It's like getting into a basket and trying to lift yourself up by the handles."

Each of the two hearers repeated this simple demonstration to at least a dozen acquaintances, who repeated it to dozens of others ; and after that John Henry Overholt could not raise another dollar to complete the Air-Motor.

Mr. Burnside's refusal had been definite and final, and he had been the last to whom the investor had applied, merely because he was undoubtedly the most close-fisted man of business of all who had invested in the invention.

Overholt saw failure before him at the very moment of success, with the not quite indifferent accompaniment of starvation. Many a man as good as he has been in the same straits, even more than once in life, and has succeeded after all, and Overholt knew this quite well, and therefore did not break down, nor despair, nor even show distinct outward signs of mental distress.

Metaphorically, he took Pandora's box to the Park, put it in a sunny corner, and sat upon it, to keep the lid down, with Hope inside, while he thought over the situation.

It was not at all a pleasant one. It is one thing to have no money to spare, but it is quite another to have none at all, and he was not far from that. He had some small possessions, but those with which he was willing to part were worth nothing, and those which would bring a little money were the expensive tools and valuable materials with which he was working. For he worked alone, profiting by his experience with the mechanic who had robbed him of one of his most profitable patents. When the idea of the Air-Motor had occurred to him he had gone into a machine-shop and had spent nearly two years in learning the use of fine tools. Then he had bought what he needed out of the money invested in his idea, and had gone to work himself, sending models of such castings as he required to different parts of the United States, that the pieces might be made independently.

He was not an accomplished workman, and he made slow progress with only his little son to help him when the boy was not at school. Often, through lack of skill, he wasted good material, and more than once he spoiled an expensive casting, and was obliged to wait till it could be made again and sent to him. Besides, he and the boy had to live, and living is dear nowadays, even in a cottage in an out-of-the-way corner of Connecticut; and he needed fire and light in abundance for his work, besides something to eat and decent clothes to wear and somebody to cook the dinner ; and when he took out his diary note-book and examined the figures on the page near the end, headed "Cash Account, November," he made out that he had three hundred and eighteen dollars and twelve cents to his credit, and nothing to come after that, and he knew that the men who had believed in him had invested, amongst them, ten thousand dollars in shares, and had paid him the money in cash in the course of the past three years, but would invest no more ; and it was all gone.

One thousand more, clear of living expenses, would do it. He was positively sure that it would be enough, and he and the boy could live on his little cash balance, by great economy, for four months, at the end of which time the Air-Motor would be perfected. But without the thousand the end of the four months would be the end of everything that was worth while in life. After that he would have to go back to teaching in order to live, and the invention would be lost, for the work needed all his time and thought.

He was a mathematician, and a very good one, besides being otherwise a man of cultivated mind and wide reading. Unfortunately for himself, or the contrary, if the invention ever succeeded, he had given himself up to higher mathematics when a young man, instead of turning his talent to account in an architect's office, a shipbuilding yard, or a locomotive shop. He could find the strain at any part of an iron frame building by the differential and integral calculus to the millionth of an ounce, but the everyday technical routine work with volumes of ready-made tables was unfamiliar and uncongenial to him; he would rather have calculated the tables themselves. The true science of mathematics is the most imaginative and creative of all sciences, but the mere application of mathematics to figures for the construction of engines, ships, or buildings is the dullest sort of drudgery.

Rather than that, he had chosen to teach what he knew and to dream of great problems at his leisure when teaching was over for the day or for the term. He had taught in a small college, and had known the rare delight of having one or two pupils who were really interested. It had been a good position, and he had married a clever New England girl, the daughter of his predecessor, who had died suddenly. They had been very happy together for years, and one boy had been born to them, whom his father insisted on christening Newton. Then Overholt had thrown up his employment for the sake of

8

getting freedom to perfect his invention, though much against his wife's advice, for she was a prudent little woman, besides being clever, and she thought of the future of the two beings she loved, and of her own, while her husband dreamed of hastening the progress of science.

Overholt came to New York because he could work better there than elsewhere, and could get better tools made, and could obtain more easily the materials he wanted. For a time everything went well enough, but when the investors began to lose faith in him things went very badly.

Then Mrs. Overholt told her husband that two could live where three could not, especially when one was a boy of twelve ; and as she would not break his heart by teasing him into giving up the invention as a matter of duty, she told him that she would support herself until it was perfected or until he abandoned it of his own accord. She was very well fitted to be a governess ; she was thirty years old and as strong as a pony, she said, and she had friends in New England who could find her a situation. He should see her whenever it was possible, she added, but there was no other way.

THE LITTLE CITY OF HOPE

Now it is not easy to find a thoroughly respectable married governess of unexceptionably good manners, who comes of a good stock and is able to teach young ladies. Such a person is a treasure to rich people who need somebody to take charge of their girls while they fly round and round the world in automobiles, seeking whom they may destroy. Therefore Mrs. Overholt obtain d a very good place before long, and when the family in which she taught had its next attack of European fever and it was decided that the girls must stay in Munich to improve their German and their music, Mrs. Overholt was offered an increase of salary if she would take them there and see to it, while their parents quartered Germany, France, Spain, and Austria at the rate of forty miles an hour, or even fifty and sixty where the roads were good. If the parents broke their necks, Mrs. Overholt would take the children home ; but this was rather in the understanding than in the agreement.

Such was the position when John Henry sat down upon the lid of Pandora's box in a sunny corner of the Central Park and reflected on Mr. Burnside's remark that " there was plenty of hope about." The inventor thought that there was not much, but such as it was, he did not mean to part with it on the ground that the man of business had called it "cheap."

He resolved his feelings into factors and simplified the form of each ; and this little mathematical operation showed that he was miserable for three reasons.

The first was that there was no money for the tangent balance of the Air-Motor, which was the final part, on which he had spent months of hard work and a hundred more than half sleepless nights.

The second was that he had not seen his wife for nearly a year, and had no idea how long it would be before he saw her again, and he was just as much in love with her as he had been fourteen years ago, when he married her.

The third, and not the least, was that Christmas was coming, and he did not see how in the world he was to make a Christmas out of nothing for Newton, seeing that a thirteen-year-old boy wants everything under the sun to cheer him up when he has no brothers and sisters, and school is closed for

THE LITTLE CITY OF HOPE

the holidays, and his mother is away from
home, and there is nobody but a dear old
tiresome father who has his nose over a lathe
all day long unless he is blinding himself with
calculating quaternions for some reason that
no lad, and very few men, can possibly understand. John Henry was obliged to confess
that hope was not much of a Christmas
present for a boy in Newton's surroundings.

For the surroundings would be dismal
in the extreme. A rickety cottage on an
abandoned Connecticut farm that is waiting
for a Bohemian emigrant to make it pay is
not a gay place, especially when two-thirds of
the house has been turned into a workshop
that smells everlastingly of smith's coal, brass
filings, and a nauseous chemical which seemed
to be necessary to the life of the Air-Motor,
and when the rest of the house is furnished
in a style that would make a condemned cell
look attractive by contrast.

Besides, it would rain or snow, and it
rarely snowed in a decent Christian manner
by Christmas. It snowed slush, as Newton
expressed it. A certain kind of snow-slush
makes nice hard snowballs, it is true, just
like stones, but when there is no other boy

12

to fight, it is no good. Overholt had once offered to have a game of snow-balling with his son on a Saturday afternoon in winter ; and the invitation was accepted with alacrity. But it was never extended again. The boy was a perfect terror at that form of diversion. Yet so distressed was Overholt at the prospect of a sad Christmas for his son that he even thought of voluntarily giving up his thin body to the torment again on the 25th of December, if that would amuse Newton and make it seem less dull for him. Good-will towards men, and even towards children, could go no further than that, even at Christmas time. At least Overholt could think of no greater sacrifice that might serve.

For what are toys to a boy of thirteen ? He wants a gun and something to kill, or he wants a boat in which he can really sail, or a live pony with a real head, a real tail, and four real legs, one at each corner. That had been Newton's definition of the desired animal when he was six years old, and some one had given him a wooden one on rockers with the legs painted on each side. Girls of thirteen can still play with dolls, and John Henry had read that, far away in ancient times, girls dedicated their dolls, with all the dolls' clothes, to Artemis on the eve of their wedding-day. But no self-respecting boy of thirteen cares a straw for anything that is not real, except an imaginary pain that will keep him away from school without cutting down his rations ; and in the invention and presentation of such fictitious suffering he beats all the doll-makers in Germany and all the playwrights and actors in the world. You must have noticed that the pain is always as far from the stomach as is compatible with probability. Toothache is a grand thing, for nobody can blame a healthy boy for eating then, if he can only bear the pain. And he can, and does, bear it nobly, though with awful faces. The little beast knows that all toothaches do not make your cheek swell. Then there is earache ; that is a splendid invention ; it goes through your head like a red-hot corkscrew with a powerful brakeman at the other end, turning it steadily—between meals. Only certain kinds of things really serve to make him stop. Ice-cream is one, and it takes a great deal of it. It is well known that ice will cool a red-hot corkscrew.

But this is a digression, for no boy ever

THE LITTLE CITY OF HOPE

has any pain at Christmas ; it is only afterwards that it comes on ; usually about ten
days.

After an hour Overholt came to the con-
clusion that he had better take Pandora's box
out to the cottage and sit on it there, since
nothing suggested itself to him, in spite of his
immense good-will to accept any suggestion
which the spirit of coming Christmas might
be kind enough to offer ; and if he could do
nothing else, he could at least work at his
machine, and try to devise some means of
constructing the tangent-balance with the
materials he had left, and perhaps, by the
time he was thoroughly grimy and the workshop smelt like the Biblical bottomless pit,
something would occur to him for Newton.

He could also write a letter to his wife, a
sort of anticipatory Christmas letter, and send
her the book he had bought as a little gift,
wrapping it in nice white paper first, tied with
a bit of pale green ribband which she had left
behind her, and which he had cherished nearly
a year, and marking it " to be opened on
Christmas morning " ; and the parcel should
then be done up securely in good brown
grocer's paper and addressed to her, and even

15

registered, so that it could not possibly be lost. It was a pretty book, and also a very excellent book, which he knew she wanted and would read often, so it was as well to take precautions. He wished that Newton wanted a book, or even two or three, or magazines with gaily coloured pictures, or anything that older or younger boys would have liked a little. But Newton was at that age which comes sooner or later to every healthy boy, and the sight of a book which he was meant to read and ought to read was infinitely worse than the ugliest old toad that ever flops out of a hollow tree at dusk, spitting poison and blinking his devilish little eyes at you when you come too near him.

Overholt had been brought up by people who lived in peace and good-will towards men, in a city where the spirit of Christmas still dwells, and sleeps most of the time, but wakens every year, like a giant of good courage and good cheer, at the sound of the merry bells across the snow, and to the sweet carol under the windows in the frosty night. The Germans say that bad men have no songs ; and we and all good fellows may say that bad people have no Christmas, and though they copy the letter they know not the spirit; and I say that a copied Christmas is no Christmas at all, because Christmas is a feast of hearts and not of poor bits of cut-down trees stuck up in sawdust and covered with lights and tinsel, even if they are hung with the most expensive gewgaws and gimcracks that ever are bought for gifts by people who are expected to give, whether they like or not. But when the heart for Christmas is there and is beating, then a very little tree will do, if there be none better to the hand.

Overholt thought so, while the train rumbled, creaked, and clattered and jerked itself along, as only local trains can, probably because they are old and rheumatic and stiff and weak in the joints, like superannuated crocodiles, though they may have once been young express trains, sleek and shiny, and quick and noiseless as bright snakes.

Overholt thought so, too ; but the trouble was that he saw not even the least little mite of a tree in sight for his boy when the 25th of December should come. And it was coming, and was only a month away ; and time is not a local train that stops at every station, and then kicks itself on a bit to stop at the next ; it is the "Fast Limited," and, what is more, it is the only one we can go by ; and we cannot get out, because it never stops anywhere.

CHAP. II

HOW A MAN AND A BOY FOUNDED THE LITTLE CITY OF HOPE.

II

HOW A MAN AND A BOY FOUNDED THE LITTLE CITY OF HOPE

OVERHOLT'S boy came home from school at the usual hour with his books buckled together in an old skate strap, which had never been very good because the leather was too soft and tore from one hole to the next ; but it served very well for the books, as no great strain was caused by an arithmetic thumbed to mushiness, a history in the same state, and a geography of which the binding gave in and doubled up from sheer weariness, while the edges were so worn that the eastern coast of China and Siberia had quite disappeared.

He was a good-looking lad, not tall for his age, but as tough as a street cat in hard training. He had short and thick brown hair, a clear complexion, his father's energetically intellectual features, though only half developed yet, a boldly-set mouth, and his mother's kindly, practical blue eyes. For surely the eyes of practical people are always quite different from those of all others ; and not many people are practical, though I never knew anybody who did not think he or she was, except pinchbeck artists, writers, and players, who are sure that since they must be geniuses, it is necessary to be Bohemians in order to show it. The really big ones are always trying to be practical, like Sir Isaac Newton when he ordered a good-sized hole to be cut in his barn door for the cat, and a little one next it for the kitten.

But Newton Overholt did not at all resemble his great namesake. He was a practical young soul, and had not yet developed the American disease which consists in thinking of two things at the same time. John Henry had it badly, for he had been thinking of the tangent-balance, his wife, his boy, and the coming Christmas, all together, since he had got home, and the three problems had got mixed and had made his head ache.

THE LITTLE CITY OF HOPE

Nevertheless he looked up from his work-table and smiled when his son came in.

"Everything all right?" he asked, with an attempt to be cheerful.

"Oh yes, fine," answered the boy, looking at the motionless model for the five-hundredth time, and sticking his hands into his pockets. "I'm only third in mathematics yet, but I'm head in everything else. I wish I had your brains, father! I'd be at the head of the arithmetic class in half a shake of a lamb's tail if I had your brains."

So far as mathematics were concerned this sounded probable to John Henry, who would have considered the speed of the tail to be a variable function of lamb, depending on the value of mother, plus or minus milk.

"Well," he said in an encouraging tone, "I never could remember geography, so it makes us even."

"I'd like to know how!" cried the boy in a tone of protest. "You could do sums, and you grew up to be a great mathematician and inventor. But what is the good of a geo-graphician, anyway? They can only make school-books. They never invent anything, do they? You can't invent geography, can

you ?   At least you can, and some boys do,
but they go to the bottom of the class like
lead.   It's safer to invent history than geography, isn't it, father ?"

Overholt's clever mouth twitched.

"It's much safer, my boy.   Almost all
historians have found it so."

"There ! I said so to-day, and now you
say just the same thing.   I don't believe one
word of ancient history.   Not—one—word !
They wrote it about their own nations, didn't
they?   All right.   Then you might just as
well expect them to tell what really happened,
as think that I'd tell on another boy in my
own school.   I must say it would be as mean
as dog pie of them if they did, but all the
same that does not make history true,
does it ?"

Newton had a practical mind.   His father,
who had not, meditated with unnecessary
gravity on the boy's point of view and said
nothing.

"For instance," continued the lad, sitting
down on the high stool before the lathe
Overholt was not using, "the charge of
Balaclava's a true story, because it's been told
by both sides ; but they all say that it did no

good, anyway, except to make poetry of. But Marathon! Nobody had a chance to say a word about it except the Greeks themselves, and they weren't going to allow that the Persians wiped up the floor with them, were they? Why should they? And if Balaclava had happened then, those Greek fellows would have told us that the Light Brigade carried the Russian guns back with them across their saddles, wouldn't they? I say, father!"

"What is it?" asked Overholt, looking up, for he had gone back to his work and was absorbed in it.

"The boys are all beginning to talk about Christmas down at the school. Now what are we going to do at Christmas? I've been wondering."

"So have I!" responded the man, laying down the screw-plate with which he was about to cut a fine thread on the end of a small brass rod for the tangent-balance. "I've been thinking about it a good deal to-day, and I haven't decided on anything."

"Let's have turkey and cranberry sauce, anyway," said Newton thoughtfully, for he had a practical mind. "And I suppose we can have ice-cream if it freezes and we can get some ice. Snow does pretty well if you pack it down tight enough with salt, and go on putting in more when it melts. Barbara doesn't make ice-cream as well as they do in New York. She puts in a lot of winter-green and too little cocoanut. But it's not so bad. We can have it, can't we, father?"

"Oh yes. Turkey, cranberry sauce, and ice-cream. But that isn't a whole Christmas!"

"I don't see what else you want, I'm sure," answered the boy thoughtfully. "I mean if it's a big turkey and there's enough ice-cream—cream-cakes, maybe. You get good cream-cakes at Bangs's, two for five cents. They're not very big, but they're all right inside—all gooey, you know. Can you think of anything else?"

"Not to eat!"

"Oh, well then, what's the matter with our Christmas? I can't see. No school and heaps of good gobbles."

"Good what?" Overholt looked at the boy with an inquiring glance, and then understood. "I see! Is that the proper word?"

"When there's lots, it is," answered Newton with conviction. "Of course, there are all sorts of things I'd like to have, but it's no good wishing you could lay Columbus's egg and hatch the American eagle, is it?[1] What would you like, father, if you could choose?"

"Three things," answered Overholt promptly. "I should like to see that wheel going round, softly and steadily, all Christmas Day. I should like to see that door open and your mother coming in."

"You bet I would too!" cried Newton, dropping from bold metaphor to vulgar vernacular. "Well, what's the third thing? You said there were three."

"I should like you to have a real, old-fashioned, glorious Christmas, my boy, such as you had when you were smaller, before we left the house where you were born."

"Oh well, you mustn't worry about me, father; if there's plenty of turkey and ice-cream and the cream-cakes, I can stand it. Mother can't come, anyhow, so that's settled, and it's no use to think about it. But the

[1] [The writer acknowledges his indebtedness for this fact in natural and national history to his aunt, Mrs. Julia Ward Howe, to whom it was recently revealed in the course of making an excellent speech.]

25

Motor—that's different. There's hope, anyway. The wheel may go round. If you didn't hope so, you wouldn't go on fussing over it, would you? You'd go and do something else. They always say hope's better than nothing."

"It's about all we shall have left for Christmas, so we may as well build as much on it as we can."

"I love building," said Newton. "I like to stand and watch a bricklayer just putting one brick on another and making the wall grow."

"Perhaps you'll turn out an architect."

"I'd like to. I never showed you my City, did I?" He knew very well that he had not, and his father looked at him inquiringly. "No. Oh well, you won't care to see it."

"Yes, I should! But I don't understand. What sort of a city do you mean?"

"Oh, it's nothing," answered the boy, affecting carelessness. "It's only a little paper city on a board. I don't believe you'd care to see it, father. Let's talk about Christmas."

"No. I want to see what you have made. Where is it? I'll go with you."

THE LITTLE CITY OF HOPE

Newton laughed.

"I'll bring it, if you really want me to. It's easy enough to carry. The whole thing's only paper!"

He left the workshop and returned before Overholt had finished cutting the thread of the screw he was making. The man turned as the boy pushed the door open with his foot, and came in carrying what had evidently once been the top of a deal table.

On the board he had built an ingenious model of a town, or part of one, but it was not finished. It was entirely made of bits of cardboard, chips of wood, the sides of match-boxes, and odds and ends of all sorts, which he picked up wherever he saw them and brought home in his pocket for his purpose. He had an immense supply of such stuff stored away, much more than he could ever use.

Overholt looked at it with admiration, but said nothing. It was the college town where he had lived so happily and hoped to live again. It was distinctly recognisable, and many of the buildings were not only cleverly made, but were coloured very like the originals. He was so much interested that he forgot to say anything.

"It's a silly thing, anyway," said Newton, disappointed by his silence. "It's like toys!"

Overholt looked up, and the boy saw his pleased face.

"It's very far from silly," he said. "I believe you're born to be a builder, boy! It's not only not silly, but it's very well done indeed!"

"I'll bet you can't tell what the place is," observed Newton, a secret joy stealing through him at his father's words.

"Know it? I should think I did, and I wish we were there now! Here's the College, and there's our house in the street on the other side of the common. The church is first-rate, it's really like it—and there's the Roman Catholic Chapel and the Public Library in Main Street."

"Why, you really do recognise the places!" cried Newton in delight. "I didn't think anybody'd know them!"

"One would have to be blind not to, if one knew the town," said Overholt. "And there's the dear old lane!" He was absorbed in the model. "And the three hickory trees, and even the little bench!"

"IT'S A SILLY THING, ANYWAY," SAID NEWTON, DISAPPOINTED BY HIS
SILENCE.

THE LITTLE CITY OF HOPE

"Why, do you remember that bench, father?"

Overholt looked up again, quickly and rather dreamily.

"Yes. It was there that I asked your mother to marry me," he said.

"Not really? Then I'm glad I put it in!"

"So am I, for the dear old time's sake and for her sake, and for yours, my boy. Tell me when you made this, and how you can remember it all so well."

The lad sat down on the high stool again before the lathe and looked through the dingy window at the scraggy trees outside, beyond the forlorn yard.

"Oh, I don't know," he said. "I kind of remember it, I suppose, because I liked it better than this. And when I first had the idea I was sitting out there in the yard looking at this board. It belongs to a broken table that had been thrown out there. And I carried it up to my room when you were out. I thought you wouldn't mind my taking it. And I picked up scraps that might be useful, and got some gum, and old Barbara made me some flour paste. It's

got green now, and it smells like thunder,
but it's good still. That's about all, I suppose. Now I'll take it away again. I keep
it in the dark closet behind my room, because
that doesn't leak when it rains."

"Don't take it away," said Overholt
suddenly. "I'll make room for it here,
and you can work at it while I'm busy, and
in the evenings I'll try and help you, and
we'll finish it together."

Newton was amazed.

"Why, father, it's playing! How can
you go to work at play? It would be so
funny! But, of course, if you really would
help me a little—you've got such lots of nice
things!"

He wistfully eyed a little coil of some
very fine steel wire which would make a
beautiful telegraph. Newton even dreamt
of making the trolley, too, in the Main Street,
but that would be a very troublesome job;
and as for the railway station, it was easy
enough to build a shed and a platform, but
what is a railway station without a train?

Overholt did not answer the boy at once,
and when he spoke there was a queer little
quaver in his voice.

THE LITTLE CITY OF HOPE

"We'll call it our little City of Hope," he said, "and perhaps we can 'go to work to play,' as you call it, so hard that Hope will really come and live in the City."

"Well," said Newton, "I never thought you'd ever care to see it! Shall I go up and get my stuff, and the gum and the flour paste, and bring them down here, father? But the flour paste smells pretty bad—it might give you a headache."

"Bring it down, my boy. My headaches don't come from such things."

"Don't they? It's true that stuff you use here's about as bad as anything, till you get used to it. What is it, anyway?"

Overholt gave him the almost unpronounceable name of some recently discovered substance, and smiled at his expression as he listened.

"If that's its name," said the boy gravely, "it sounds like the way it smells. I wonder what a skunk's name is in science. But the flour paste's pretty bad too. You'll see!"

He went off, and his father finished cutting the little screw while he was gone, and then turned to look at the model again, and became absorbed in tracing the well-

known streets and trying to recall the shops
and houses in each, and the places where his
friends had lived, and no doubt lived still,
for college towns do not change as fast as
others. He was amazed at the memory the
boy had shown for details ; if the lad had not
yet developed any special talent, he had at
least proved that he possessed one of those
natural gifts which are sometimes alone
enough to make success. The born builder's
eye is like an ear for music, a facility for
languages, or the power of drawing from
nature ; all the application in the world will
not do in years what any one of these does
instantly, spontaneously, instinctively, without
the smallest effort. You cannot make talent
out of a combination of taste and industry.
You cannot train a cart-horse to trot a mile
in a little over a minute.

Newton returned, bringing his materials,
to describe which would be profitless, if it
were possible. He had everything littered
together in two battered deal candle-boxes,
including the broken soup-plate containing
the flour paste, a loathely, mouldering little
mess that diffused a nauseous odour, distinctly perceptible through that of the

THE LITTLE CITY OF HOPE

unpronounceable chemical on which the Air-Motor was to depend for its existence.

The light outside was failing in the murky November air, and Overholt lit the big reflecting lamp that hung over the work-table. There was another above the lathe, for no gas or electricity was to be had so far from the town, and one of old Barbara's standing causes of complaint against Overholt was his reckless use of kerosene—she thought it would be better if he had more fat turkeys and rump-steaks and less light.

So the man and the boy "went to work to play" at building the City of Hope, for at least an hour before supper and half an hour after it, almost every day; and with the boy's marvellous memory and the father's skill, and the delicious profusion of fresh material which Newton kept finding in every corner of the workshop, it grew steadily, till it was a little work of art in its way. There were the ups and downs, the crooked old roads and lanes and the straight new streets, the little wooden cottages and the big brick houses, and there was the grassy common with its trees and its tiny iron railing; and John Henry easily made posts to carry the

33

trolley wires, which had seemed an impossible dream to the boy, beyond all realisation ; and one day, when the inventor seemed farther from the tangent-balance than ever, he spent a whole afternoon in making a dozen little trolley-cars that ran on real wheels, made by sawing off little sections from a lead pencil, which is the best thing in the world for that, because the lead comes out and leaves nice round holes for the axles. When the first car was painted red and yellow and ran up and down Main Street, guided by the wire above and only needing one little artificial push to send it either way, it looked so real that the boy was in ecstasies of delight.

"It's worth while to be a great inventor to be able to make things like that!" he cried, and Overholt was as much pleased by the praise as an opera singer is who is called out three times before the curtain after the first act.

So the little City of Hope grew, and they both felt that Hope herself was soon coming to dwell therein, if she had not come already.

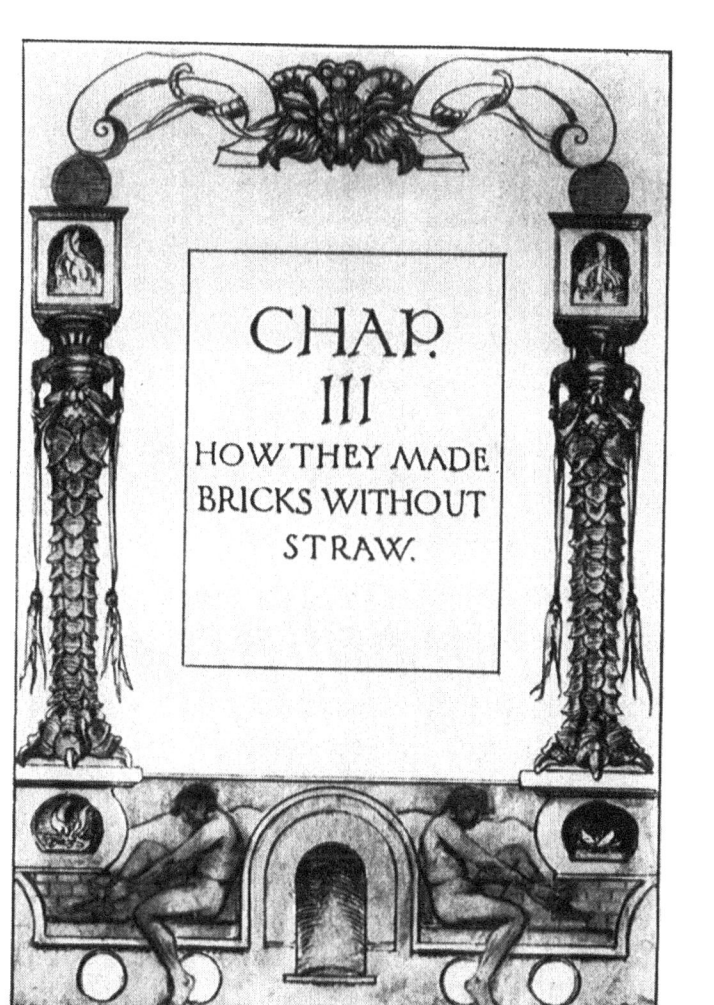

CHAP.
III
HOW THEY MADE
BRICKS WITHOUT
STRAW.

III

BUT then something happened ; for Overholt
was tormented by the vague consciousness
of a coming idea, so that he had headaches
and could not sleep at night. It flashed
upon him at last one evening when Newton
was in bed and he was sitting before his
Motor, wishing he had the thousand dollars
which would surely complete it, even if he
used the most expensive materials in the
market.

The idea which developed suddenly in all
its clearness was that he had made one of the
most important parts of the machine exactly
the converse of what it should be ; what was
on the right should have been on the left,
and what was down should certainly have

35

been up. Then the engine would work, even if the tangent-balance were a very poor affair indeed.

The particular piece of brass casting which was the foundation of that part had been made in New York, and, owing to the necessity for its being finished very accurately and machine planed and turned, it had cost a great deal of money. Already it had been made and spoilt three times over, and now it was perfectly clear that it must be cast over again in a reversed form. It was quite useless to make the balance yet, for it would be of no use till the right casting was finished ; it would have to be reversed too, and the tangent would apply to a reversed curve.

He had no money for the casting, but even before trying to raise the cash it was necessary to make the wooden model. He could do that, and he set to work to sketch the drawing within five minutes after the idea had once flashed upon him. As his eye followed the lines made by his pencil, he became more and more convinced that he was right. When the rough sketch was done he looked up at the engine. Its familiar features seemed to be drawn into a diabolical grimace of contempt at his stupidity, and it looked as if it were conscious and wanted to throw the wrongly-made piece at his head. But he was overwrought just then and could have fancied any folly.

He rose, shook himself, and then took a long pull at a black bottle that always stood on a shelf. When a man puts a black bottle to his lips, tips it up, and takes down several good pulls almost without drawing breath, most people suppose that he is a person of vicious habits. In Overholt's case most people would have been wrong. The black bottle contained cold tea ; it was strong, but it was only tea, and that is the finest drink in the world for an inventor or an author to work on. When I say an author I mean a poor writer of prose, for I have always been told that all poets are either mad, or bad, or both. Many of them must be bad, or they could not write such atrocious poems ; but madness is different ; perhaps they read their own verses.

When Overholt had swallowed his cold tea, he got out his drawing materials, stretched a fresh sheet of thick draughtsman's paper on the board, and sat down between the Motor that would not move and the little city in which Hope had taken lodgings for a while, and he went to work with ruler, scale and dividers, and the hard wood template for drawing the curves he had constructed for the tangent-balance by a very abstruse mathematical calculation. That was right, at all events, only, as it was to be reversed, he laid it on the paper with the under-side up.

He worked nearly all night to finish the drawing, slept two hours in a battered Shaker rocking-chair by the fire, woke in broad daylight, drank more cold tea, and went at once to his lathe, for the new piece was in the nature of a cylinder, and a good deal of the work could be done by turning.

The chisel and the lathe seemed to be talking to each other over the block of wood, and what they said rang like a tune in John Henry's head.

"Bricks without straw, bricks without straw, bricks without straw," repeated the lathe regularly, at each revolution, and when it said "bricks" the treadle was up, and when it said "straw" the treadle was down, for of course it was only a foot lathe, though a good one. "Sh—sh—sh—ever so much

better than no bricks at all—sh—sh—sh,"
answered the sharp chisel as it pressed and
bit the wood, and made a little irregular
clattering when it was drawn away, and then
came forward against the block again with a
long hushing sound ; and Overholt was in-
clined to accept its opinion, and worked on
as if an obliging brassfounder were waiting
outside to take the model away at once and
cast it for nothing, or at least on credit.

But no such worthy and confiding manu-
facturer appeared, even on the evening of the
second day, when the wooden model was
beautifully finished and ready for the foundry.
While the inventor was busy, Newton had
worked alone in a corner when he had time
to spare from his lessons, but he understood
what was going on, and he did not accom-
plish much beyond painting the front of the
National Bank in the City of Hope and
planning a possible Wild West Show to be
set up on the outskirts ; the tents would be easy
to make, but the horses were beyond his skill,
or his father's ; it would not be enough that
they should have a leg at each corner and a
head and a tail.

He understood well enough what was the

matter, for he had seen similar things happen before. A pessimist is defined to be a person who has lived with an optimist, and every inventor is that. Poor Newton had seen that particular part of the engine spoiled and made over three times, and he understood perfectly that it was all wrong again and must be cast once more. But he kept his reflections to himself and tried to think about the City of Hope.

"I wish," said John Henry, sitting down opposite the boy at last, and looking at what he had done, "that the National Bank in Main Street were real!"

He eyed it wistfully.

"Oh well," answered the boy, "we couldn't rob it, because that's stealing, so I don't see what particular good it would do!"

"Perhaps the business people in the City of Hope would be different from the bankers in New York," observed Overholt, thoughtfully.

"I don't believe it, father," Newton answered in a sceptical tone. "If they were bankers they'd be rich, and you remember the sermon Sunday before last, about it's being easier for the camel to get through the rich man—no, which is it? I forget. It doesn't matter, anyway, because we can imagine any kind of people we choose in our City, can't we? Say, father, what's the matter? Are you going to cast that piece over again? That'll be the fourth time, won't it?"

"It would be, my boy, but it won't be. They won't cast it for nothing, and I cannot raise the money. You cannot make bricks without straw."

He looked steadily down at the tiny front of the Bank in Main Street, and a hungry look came into his eyes.

But Newton had a practical mind, even at thirteen.

"I was thinking," he said presently. "It looks as if we were going to get stuck some day. What are we going to do then, father? I was thinking about it just now. How are we going to get anything to eat if we have no money?"

"I shall have to go back to teaching mathematics for a living, I suppose."

"And give up the Motor?" Newton had never yet heard him suggest such a thing.

"Yes," Overholt answered in a low tone; and that was all he said.

THE LITTLE CITY OF HOPE

"Oh, that's ridiculous. You'd just die, that's all!"

Newton stared at the engine that was a failure. It looked as if it ought to work, he thought, with its neat cylinders, its polished levers, its beautifully designed gear. It stood under a big case made of thick glass plates set in an iron frame with a solid top; a chain ran through two cast-iron wheels overhead to a counterpoise in the corner, by which device it was easily raised and lowered. The Motor was a very expensive affair, and had to be carefully protected from dust and all injury, though it was worth nothing at present except for old brass and iron, unless the new part could be made.

"Come, my boy, let's think of something more cheerful!" Overholt said, making an effort to rouse himself and concentrate his attention on the paper model. "Christmas is coming in three weeks, you know, and it will come just the same in the little City. I'm sure the people will decorate their houses and the church. Of course we cannot see the insides of the houses, but in Boston they put wreaths in the windows. And we'll

SO THEY WORKED TOGETHER STEADILY.

have a snowstorm, just as we used to have, and we can clear it away afterwards ! Wasn't there a holly tree somewhere near the College ? You haven't put that in yet. You have no idea how cheerful it will look ! To-morrow we'll find a very small sprig with berries on it, and plant it just in the right place. I'm sure you remember where it stood."

"Real leaves would be too big," observed the boy. "They wouldn't look right. Of course, one could cut the branches out of tin and paint 'em green with red spots, and stick them into a twig for the trunk. But it's rather hard to do."

"Let's try," said Overholt. "I've got some fine chisels and some very thin brass, but I don't think I could draw the branches as well as you could."

"Oh, I can draw them something like, if you'll only cut 'em out," the boy answered cheerfully. "Come on, father ! Who says we can't make bricks without straw ? I'll bet anything we can ! "

So they worked together steadily, and for an hour or two the inventor was so busy in cutting out tiny branches of imaginary holly with a very small chisel that he did not look once at the plate glass from which his engine seemed to be grinning at him, in fiendish delight over his misfortunes. There were times when he was angry with it, outright, as if it knew what he was doing and did not mean to give in to him and let itself be invented.

But now the tune of the lathe and the chisel still ran on in his head, for he had heard it through two whole days and could not get rid of it.

"Bricks without straw, bricks without straw!" repeated the lathe viciously. "Ever so much better than no bricks at all, sh—sh—sh!" answered the chisel, gibbering and hissing like an idiot.

"You will certainly be lying on straw before long, and then I suppose you'll wish you had something else!" squeaked the little chisel with which he was cutting out holly leaves, as it went through the thin plates into the wood of the bench under each push of his hand.

The things in the workshop all seemed to be talking to him together, and made his head ache.

"I had a letter from your mother to-day,"

he said, because it was better to hear his own voice say anything than to listen to such depressing imaginary conversations. " I'm sorry to say she sees no chance of getting home before the spring."

" I don't know where you'd put her if she came here," answered the practical Newton. " Your room leaks when it rains, and so does mine. You two would have to sleep in the parlour. I guess it'll be better if she doesn't come now."

" Oh, for her, far better," assented Overholt. " They've got a beautiful flat in Munich, and everything they can possibly think of. Your mother's only complaint, so far as that goes, is that those girls are com·-pletely spoilt by too much luxury ! "

" What is luxury, exactly, father ? " asked Newton, who always wanted to know things.

" I shall never know myself, and perhaps you never will either ! " The wretched inventor tried to laugh. " But that's no answer to your question, is it ? I suppose luxury means always having twice as much of everything as you can possibly use, and having it about ten times as fine and expensive as other people can afford."

THE LITTLE CITY OF HOPE

"I don't see any use in that," said the boy. "Now I know just how much turkey and cranberry sauce and ice-cream I really need, and if I get just a little more than that, it's Christmas. I don't mean much more, but about half a helping. I know all about proverbs. Haven't I copied millions of 'em in learning to write. One reason why it's so slow to learn is that the things you have to write are perfect nonsense. 'Enough is as good as a feast!' All I can say is, the man who made that proverb never had a feast, or he'd have known better! This green paint doesn't dry very quick, father. We'll have to wait till to-morrow before we put in the red spots for the berries. I wish I had some little red beads. They'd stick on the wet paint now, like one o'clock."

There were no red beads, so he rose to go to bed. When he had said good-night and had reached the door, he stopped and looked back again.

"Say, father, haven't you anything you can sell to get some more money for the Motor?"

John Henry shook his weary head and smiled sadly.

THE LITTLE CITY OF HOPE

" Nothing that would bring nearly enough
to pay for the casting," he answered. " Don't
worry about it, boy. Leave that to me—I'm
used to it. Go to bed and sleep, and you'll
feel like an Air-Motor yourself in the
morning ! "

" That's the worst of it," returned the
boy. " Just to sit there under a glass case
and have you take care of me and do nothing,
like a girl. That's the way I feel sometimes."

He shook his young head quite as gravely
as the inventor had shaken his own, and went
quietly to bed without saying anything more.

" I don't know what to do, I'm sure," he
said to himself as he got into bed, " but I'm
sure there's something. Maybe I'll dream
it, and then I'll do just the contrary and it'll
come all right."

But boys of practical minds and sound
bodies do not dream at all, unless it be after
a feast, and most of them can stand even that
without having nightmare, unless two feasts
come near together, like Christmas and a
birthday within the week.

A great-uncle of mine was once taken for
a clergyman at a public dinner nearly a
hundred years ago, and he was asked to say

grace ; he was a good man, and also practical, and had a splendid appetite, but he was not eloquent, and this is what he said :—

" The Lord give us appetites to enjoy, and strength to digest ALL the good things set before us. Amen ! "

And everybody said " Amen " very cheerfully and fell to.

CHAP.
IV
HOW THERE WAS
A FAMINE IN THE
CITY

IV

It rained in New York and it "snowed slush" in Connecticut, after its manner, and the world was a very dreary place, especially all around the dilapidated cottage where everything was going to pieces, including John Henry Overholt's last hopes.

If he had been alone in the world he would have taken his small cash balance and his model to the foundry, quite careless as to whether he ever got a meal again until the Motor worked. But there was the boy to be thought of, and desperate as the unhappy inventor was, he would not starve his son as well as himself. He was quite sure of his little balance, though he had never had any head for figures of that sort. It was an easy

49

affair in his eyes to handle the differential calculus, which will do anything, metaphorically speaking, from smashing a rock as flat and thin as a postage stamp, to regulating an astronomical clock ; but to understand the complication of a pass-book and a bank account was a matter of the greatest possible difficulty. Newton would have done it much better, though he could not get to the head of his class in arithmetic. That is the difference between being an inventor and having a practical mind. As for Mrs. Overholt, she was perfectly wonderful at keeping accounts; but then she had been taught a great many things, from music and drawing to compound interest and double entry, and she had been taught them all just so far as to be able to do them nicely without understanding at all what she did ; which is sound modern education, and no mistake. The object of music is to make a cheerful noise, which can be done very well without pencil and paper and the rules of harmony.

But Overholt could neither make a cheerful noise, nor draw a holly leaf, nor speak French, nor even understand a pass-book, though he had invented an Air-Motor which would not work, but was a clear evidence of genius. The only business idea he had was to make his little balance last as long as possible, in spite of the terrible temptation to take it and offer it to the founder as a cash advance, if only he might have his piece of casting done. Where the rest of the money would come from he did not know ; probably out of the Motor. It looked so easy ; but there was the boy, and it might happen that there would be no dinner for several days.

On the first of December he cashed a cheque in the town, as usual ; and he paid Barbara's wages and the coal merchant, and the month's bill for kerosene, and the butcher and the grocer, and the baker, and that was practically all ; and he went to bed that night feeling that whatever happened there was a whole month before another first came round, and he owed no one anything more for the present, and Newton would not starve, and could have his Christmas turkey, if it was to be the last he ever ate, poor boy.

On the morning of December third it was still snowing slush, though it was more like real snow now, and the air was much colder ; and by and by, when Overholt had read a letter that Barbara brought him, he felt so terribly cold all at once that his teeth chattered, and then he was so hot that the perspiration ran down his forehead, and he steadied himself against the heavy glass case of the Motor a moment and then almost tumbled into a sitting posture on the stool before his worktable, and his head fell forward on his hands, as if he were fainting.

The letter said that his account was overdrawn to the extent of three hundred and fifty-two dollars and thirteen cents, including the cheque he had drawn on the thirty-first, and would he please make a deposit at his earliest convenience?

It had been just a little mistake in arithmetic, that was all. He had started with the wrong balance in his note-book, and what he thought was credit was debit, but the bank where he had kept all the money that had been put up for the Motor, had wished to be friendly and good-natured to the great inventor and had not returned his cheques with N.G. on them ; and if his attention had already been called to his deficit, he must have forgotten to open the letter. Like all men who are much talked of in the newspapers, though they may be as poor as Job's turkey, he received a great many circulars addressed by typewriter, and the only letters he really cared for were from his wife, so that when he was very hard at work or much pre-occupied the others accumulated somewhere in the workshop, and were often forgotten.

What was perfectly clear this morning was that starvation was sitting on the door-step and that he had no moral right whatever to the dinner Barbara was already beginning to cook, nor to another to-morrow, nor to any more ; for he was a proud man, and ashamed of debt, though he mixed up debit and credit so disgracefully.

He sat there half an hour, as he had let himself fall forward, only moving a little, so that his forehead rested on his arm instead of his hands, because that was a little more comfortable, and just then he did not want to see anything, least of all the Motor. When he rose at last the sleeve of his coat was all wet with the perspiration from his forehead. He left the workshop, half shut-ting his eyes in order not to see the Motor ; he was sure the thing was grinning at him behind the plate glass. It had two round

brass valves near the top that looked like
yellow eyeballs, and a lever at the bottom
with double arms and a cross-bar, which
made him think of an iron jaw when he was
in one of his fits of nervous depression.

But John Henry Overholt was a man, and
an honest one. He went straight to the
writing-table in the next room and sat down,
and though his hand shook, he wrote a clear
and manly letter to the President of the
College where he had taught so well, stating
his exact position, acknowledging the failure
of his invention, and asking help to find
immediate employment as a teacher, even in
the humblest capacity which would afford
bread for his boy and himself. Presidents
and principals of colleges are in constant
communication with other similar institutions,
and generally know of vacant positions.

When he had written his letter and read
it over carefully, Overholt looked at his time-
table, got his hat, coat, and umbrella, and
trudged off through the slushy snow to the
station, on his way to New York.

It was raining there, but it was not dismal;
hurry, confusion, and noise can never be that.
He had not been in the city since the day

TRUDGED OFF THROUGH THE SLUSHY SNOW TO THE STATION, ON HIS
WAY TO NEW YORK.

when he made his last attempt to raise money,
and in his present state the contrast was over-
whelming. The shopkeepers would have told
him that it was a dull day for business, and
that the rain was costing them hundreds of
dollars every hour, because there are a vast
number of people who buy things within the
month before Christmas, if it is convenient
and the weather is fine, but will not take the
trouble if the weather is bad ; and afterwards
they are so glad to have saved their money
that they buy nothing of that sort till the
following year. For Christmas shopping is
largely a matter of temptation on the one side
and of weakness on the other, and you cannot
tempt a man to buy your wares if he will not
even go out and look at your shop window.
At Christmas time every shopkeeper turns
into a Serpent, with a big S and a supply of
apples varying, with his capital, from a paper-
bagful to a whole orchard, and though the
ladies are the more easily tempted, nine
generous men out of ten show no more
sense just at that time than Eve herself did.
The very air has temptation in it when they
see the windows full of pretty things and
think of their wives and their children and

THE LITTLE CITY OF HOPE

their old friends. Even misers relax a little
then, and a famous statesman, who was some-
what close-fisted in his day, is reported to have
given his young coloured servant twenty-five
cents on Christmas Eve, telling him to go out
to Mount Auburn Cemetery and see where
the great men of New England lie buried.
And the man, I believe, went there ; but he
was an African, and the spirit of Christmas
was not in his race, for if it had moved him
he would have wasted that money on cream-
cakes and cookies, reflecting that the buried
worthies of Massachusetts could not tell tales
on him.

Overholt went down town to the bank
where he kept his account and explained his
little mistake very humbly, and asked for
time to pay up. The teller looked at him as
if he were an escaped lunatic, but on account
of his great reputation as an inventor he was
shown to the desk of one of the partners,
which stood in a corner of the vast place,
where one could converse confidentially if one
did not speak above a whisper ; but the
stenographer girl could hear even whispering
distinctly, and perhaps she sometimes took
down what she heard, if the partner made a

56

THE LITTLE CITY OF HOPE

signal to her by carelessly rolling his pencil across his table.

The partner whom Overholt saw was not ill-natured, and besides, it was near Christmas, and he had been poor himself when he was young. If Overholt would kindly sign a note at sixty days for the overdraft it would be all right. The banker was sorry he could not authorise him to overdraw any further, but it was strictly against the rules, an exception had been made because Mr. Overholt was such a well-known man, and so forth. But the inventor explained that he had not meant to ask any favour, and had come to explain how he had made such a strange mistake. The banker, like the teller, thought that a man who could not count money must be mad, but was too civil, or too good-natured, to say so.

Overholt signed the note, thanked him warmly, and went away. He and his old umbrella looked very dejected as he left the building and dived into the stream of men in the street, but if he had paid any attention to his fellow-beings he would have seen here and there a number who looked quite as unhappy as he did. He had come all the way from the country expressly to explain his error, and had been in the greatest haste to get down town and have the interview over. To go home with the prospect of trying to eat a dinner that would be cold, and of sitting in his workshop all the afternoon just to stare at his failure until Newton came home, was quite another matter. If the weather had been less disagreeable he would have gone to the Central Park, to sit in a quiet corner and think matters over.

As that seemed out of the question, he walked from the bank to Forty-Second Street, taking an hour and a half over it. It was better to go on foot than to sit in a car facing a dozen or twenty strangers, who would wonder why he looked so miserable. Sensitive people always fancy that everybody is looking at them and criticising them, when in fact no one cares a straw how they look or what they do.

Then, too, he was in such a morbid state of mind about his debt that it looked positively wrong to spend five cents on a car-fare ; even the small change in his pocket was not his own, and that, and hundreds of dollars besides, must be paid back in sixty days.

Otherwise he supposed he would be bankrupt, which, to his simple mind, meant disgrace as well as ruin.

It had stopped raining before he reached Grace Church, and as he crossed Madison Square the sun shone out, the wind had veered to the west, and the sky was clearing all round. The streets had seemed full before, but they were positively choking with people now. The shops drew them in and blew them out again with much less cash about them, as a Pacific whale swallows water and spouts it out, catching the little fish by thousands with his internal whalebone fishing-net. But, unlike the fishes, the people were not a whit less pleased. On the contrary, there was something in the faces of almost all that is only seen once a year in New York, and then only for certain hours ; and that is real good-will. For whatever the most home-loving New Yorker may say of his own great city, good-will to men is not its dominant characteristic, nor peace its most remarkable feature.

Even poor Overholt, half crazy with disappointment and trouble, could not help noticing the difference between the expressions of the men he had seen down town and of those who were thronging the shops and the sidewalks in Fifth Avenue. In Wall Street and adjacent Broadway a great many looked like more or less discontented birds of prey looking out for the next meal, and a few might have been compared to replete vultures ; but here all those who were not alone were talking with their companions, and many were smiling, and now and then a low laugh was heard, which is a very rare thing in Fifth Avenue, though you may often hear children laughing in the Park and sometimes in the cross streets up-town.

Then there was another eagerness in the faces, that was not for money, but was the anticipation of giving pleasure before long, and of being pleased too ; and that is a great part of the Christmas spirit, if it is not the spirit itself. It is doubtless more blessed to give than to receive, but the receiving is very delightful, and it is cruel to teach children that they must not look forward to having pretty presents. What is Christmas Day to a happy child but a first glimpse of heaven on earth?

Overholt glanced at the faces of the passersby with a sort of vague surprise, wondering why they looked so happy ; and then he remembered what they were doing, and all at once his heart sank like lead. What was to become of the turkey and the ice-cream on which Newton had built his hopes for Christmas? Would there be any dinner at all? Or any one to cook it ? How could he go and get things which he would not be able to pay for on the first of next month, exactly a week after the feast? His imagination could glide lightly over three weeks of starvation, but at the thought of his boy's disappointment everything went to pieces, the present, the future, everything. He would have walked all the way down town again to beg for a loan of only a few dollars, enough for that one Christmas dinner ; but he knew from the banker's face that such a request would be refused, as such, and he dreaded in his misery lest the money should be offered him as a charity.

He got home at last, weary and wretched, and then for the first time he remembered the letter he had written asking for employment as a teacher. He had been a very good one, and the College had been sorry to lose

him ; in two days he might get an answer ;
all hope was not gone yet, at least not quite
all, and his spirits revived a little. Besides,
the weather was fine now, even in Connecticut ; there would be a sharp frost in the
night, and Newton would soon get some
skating.

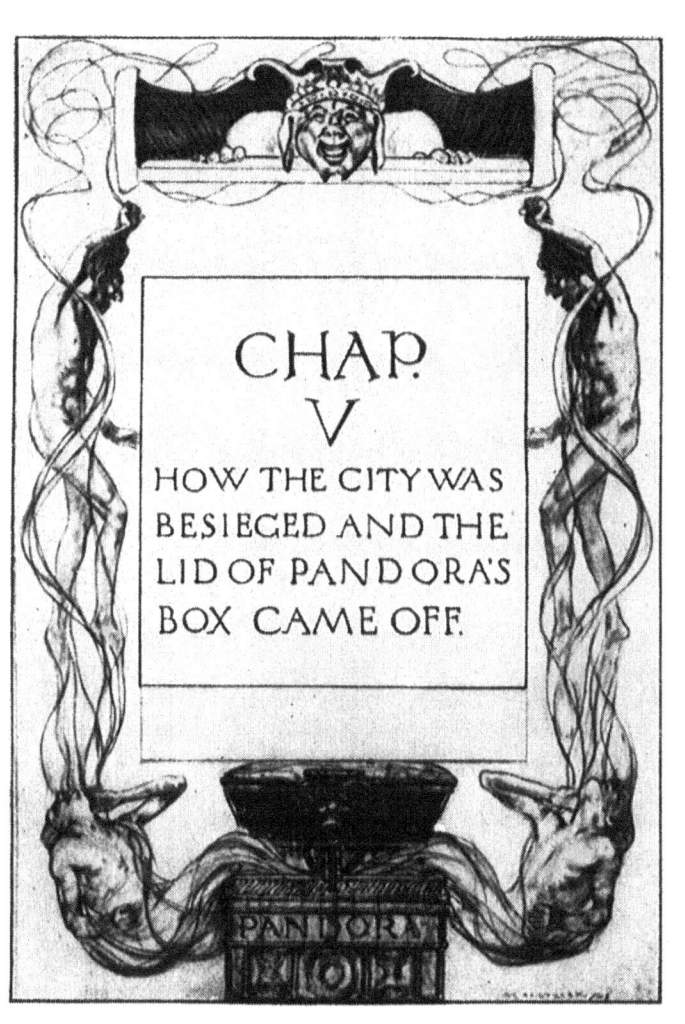

CHAP.
V

HOW THE CITY WAS
BESIEGED AND THE
LID OF PANDORA'S
BOX CAME OFF.

V

HOW THE CITY WAS BESIEGED AND THE LID OF PANDORA'S BOX CAME OFF

ALMOST the worst part of it was that he had to tell his boy about his dreadful mistake, and that it was all over with the Motor and with everything, and that until he could get something to do they were practically starving ; and that he could not possibly see how there was ever to be ice-cream for Christmas, let alone such an expensive joy as a turkey.

He knew that Newton would not pucker up his mouth and screw his eyes to keep the tears in, like a girl ; and he was quite sure that the boy would not reproach him for having been so careless. He might not seem to care very much, but he would be terribly disappointed ; that was the worst of it all, next to owing money that he had no hope of paying. Indeed, he hardly knew which hurt him more than the other, for the disgrace of debt, as he called it, was all his own, but the bitter disappointment was on Newton too.

The latter listened in silence till his father had finished, and his boyish face was preternaturally thoughtful.

"I've seen boys make just such mistakes at the blackboard," he observed in a tone of melancholy reflection. "And they generally catch it afterwards too," he added. "It's natural."

"I've 'caught it,'" Overholt answered. "You have too, my dear boy, though you didn't make the mistake—that's not just."

"Well, father, I don't know what we're going to do, but something has got to be done right away, and we've got to find out what it is."

"Thank goodness you're not a girl!" cried Overholt fervently.

"I'm glad too; only, if I were one, I should most likely die young and go to heaven, and you'd have me off your mind all right. The girls always do in story-books."

THE LITTLE CITY OF HOPE

He made this startling and general obser-
vation quite naturally. Of course girls died
and went to heaven when there was nothing
to eat ; he secretly thought it would be
better if more of them did, even without
starvation.

"Let's work, anyhow," he added, as his
father said nothing. "Maybe we'll think of
something while we're building that railroad
depôt. Don't you suppose that now you've
got so far the Motor would keep while you
taught, and you could go at it again in the
vacations ? That's an idea, father, come
now ! "

He was already in his place before the
board on which the little City was built, and
his eyes were fixed on the lines his father
had drawn as a plan for the station and the
diverging tracks. But Overholt did not sit
down. His usual place was opposite the
Motor, where he could see it, but he did not
want to look at it now.

"Change seats with me, boy," he said.
"I cannot stand the sight of it. I suppose
I'm imaginative. All this has upset me a
good deal."

He wished he had the lad's nerves, the

solid nerves of hungry and sleepy thirteen.
Newton got up at once and changed places,
and for a few minutes Overholt tried to concentrate his mind on the little City, but it
was of no use. If he did not think of the
Motor, he thought of what was much worse,
for the little streets and models of the familiar
places brought back the cruel memory of
happier things so vividly that it was torment.
All his faculties of sensation were tense and
vibrating ; he could hear his wife's gentle
and happy voice, her young girl's voice, when
he looked at the little bench in the lane
where he had asked her to marry him, and
an awful certainty came upon him that he
was never to hear her speak again on this
side of the grave ; there was the house they
had lived in ; from that window he had looked
out on a May morning at the budding trees
half an hour after his boy had been born ;
there, in the pretty garden, the young mother
had sat with her baby in the lovely June days
—it was full of her. Or if he looked at the
College, he knew every one of the steps, and
the entrance, and the tall windows of the
lecture-rooms, where he had taught so con-
tentedly, year after year, till the terrible

66

Motor had taken possession of him, the thing that was driving him mad; and, strangely enough, what hurt him most and brought drops of perspiration to his forehead was the National Bank in Main Street; it made him remember his debt, and that he had no money at all—nothing whatsoever but the few dollars in his pocket left after paying the bills on the first of the month.

"It's of no use!" he cried, suddenly rising and turning away. "I cannot stand it. I'm sorry, but it's too awful!"

Never before had he felt so thoroughly ashamed of himself. He was breaking down before his son, to whom he knew he ought to be setting an example of fortitude and common sense. He had forgotten the very names of such qualities; the mere thought of Hope, whenever it crossed his mind, mocked him maddeningly, and he hated the little City for the name he had given it. Hope was his enemy since she had left him, and he was hers; he could have found it in his heart to crush the poor little paper town to pieces, and then to split up the very board itself for firewood.

The years that had been so full of belief

were all at once empty, and the memory of them rang hollow and false, because Hope had cheated him, luring him on, only to forsake him at the great moment. Every hour he had spent on the work had been misspent; he saw it all now, and the most perfect of his faultless calculations only proved that science was a blatant fraud and a snare that had cost him all he had, his wife, his boy's future, and his own self-respect. How could he ever look at his wretched failure again? How could he sit down opposite the son he had cheated, and who was going to starve with him, and play with a little City of Hope, when Hope herself was the lying enemy that had coaxed him to the destruction of his family and to his own disgrace? As for teaching again, who ever got back a good place after he had voluntarily given it up for a wild dream! Men who had such dreams were not fit to teach young men in any case! That was the answer he would get by post in a day or two.

Newton watched his father anxiously, for he had heard that people sometimes went mad from disappointment and anxiety. The pale intellectual face wore a look of horror, as if the dark eyes saw some dreadful sight ; the thin figure moved nervously, the colourless lips twitched, the lean fingers opened and shut spasmodically on nothing. It was enough to scare the boy, who had always known his father gentle, sweet-tempered, and hopeful even under failure ; but Overholt was quite changed now, and looked as if he were either very ill or very crazy.

It is doubtful whether boys ever love their fathers as most of them love their mothers at one time, or all their lives. The sort of attachment there often is between father and son is very different from that, and both feel that it is ; there is more of alliance and friendship in it than of anything like affection, even when it is at its best, with a strong instinct to help one another and to stand by each other in a fight.

Newton Overholt did not feel any sympathetic thrill of pain for his father's sufferings ; not in the least ; he would perhaps have said that he was "sorry for him" without quite knowing what that meant. But he was very strongly moved to help him in some way, seeing that he was evidently getting the worst of it in a big fight. Newton soon became entirely possessed by the idea that " something ought to be done," but what it was he did not know.

The lid of Pandora's box had flown open and had come off suddenly after smashing the hinges, and Hope had flown out of the window. The boy thought it was clearly his duty to catch her and get her into prison again, and then to nail down the lid. He had not the smallest doubt that this was what he ought to do, but the trouble lay in finding out how to do it, a little difficulty that humanity has faced for a good many thousand years. On the other hand, if he failed, as seemed probable, he was almost sure that his father would fall ill and die, or go quite mad in a few hours. He wished his mother were there ; she would have known how to cheer the desperate man, and could probably have made him smile in a few minutes without really doing anything at all. Those were the things women could do very well, the boy thought, and they ought always to be at hand to do them when wanted. He himself could only sit there and pretend to be busy, as children mostly do when they see their elders in trouble. But that made him wild.

THE LITTLE CITY OF HOPE

"I say, father," he broke out suddenly, "can't I do anything? Try and think!"

"That's what I'm trying to do," answered Overholt, sitting down at last on the stool before the work-bench and staring at the wall, with his back turned to his son. "But I can't! There's something wrong with my head."

"You want to see a doctor," said the boy. "I'll go and see if I can get one of them to come out here." He rose as if to go at once.

"No! Don't!" cried Overholt, much distressed by the mere suggestion. "He could only tell me to rest, and take exercise and sleep at night and not worry!" He laughed rather wildly. "He would tell me not to worry! They always say that! A doctor would tell a man 'not to worry' if he was to be hanged the next morning!"

"Well," said Newton philosophically, "I suppose a man who's going to be hung needn't worry much, anyway. He's got the front seat at the show and nothing particular to do!"

This was sound, so far as it went, but insufficient as consolation. Overholt either did not hear, or paid no heed to the boy. He left the room a moment later without shutting the door, and threw himself down on the old black horsehair sofa in the parlour. Presently the lad rose again and covered up the City of Hope with the big brown paper case he had made to fit down over the board and keep the dust off.

"This isn't your day," he observed as he did so, and the remark was certainly addressed to the model of the town.

He went into the other room and stood beside his father, looking down at his drawn face and damp forehead.

"Say, father, really, isn't there anything I can do to help?"

Overholt answered with an effort. "No, my boy, there's nothing, thank you. You cannot find money to pay my debts, can you?"

"Have you got no money at all?" asked Newton, very gravely.

"Four or five dollars! That's all! That's all you and I have got left in the world to live on, and even that's not mine!"

His voice shook with agony, and he raised one hand to his forehead, not dramatically, as

"SAY, FATHER, REALLY, ISN'T THERE ANYTHING I CAN DO TO HELP?"

many foreigners would do, but quietly and firmly, and he pressed and kneaded the surface as if he were trying to push his brains back into the right place, so that they would work, or at least keep quiet. After that answer Newton was too sensible to ask any more questions, and perhaps he was also a little afraid to, because questions might make his father worse.

"Well," he said vaguely, "if I can't work at the City I suppose I may as well go out before it's dark and take a look at the pond. It's going to freeze hard to-night, and maybe there'll be black ice that'll bear by to-morrow."

Overholt was glad to be left alone, for he could not help being ashamed of having broken down so completely before the boy, and he felt that he could not recover his self-control unless he were left to himself.

He heard Newton go up the rickety stairs to his own room, where he seemed to be rummaging about for some time, judging from the noises overhead ; then the strong shoes clattered on the staircase again, the house door was opened and shut, and the boy was off.

.

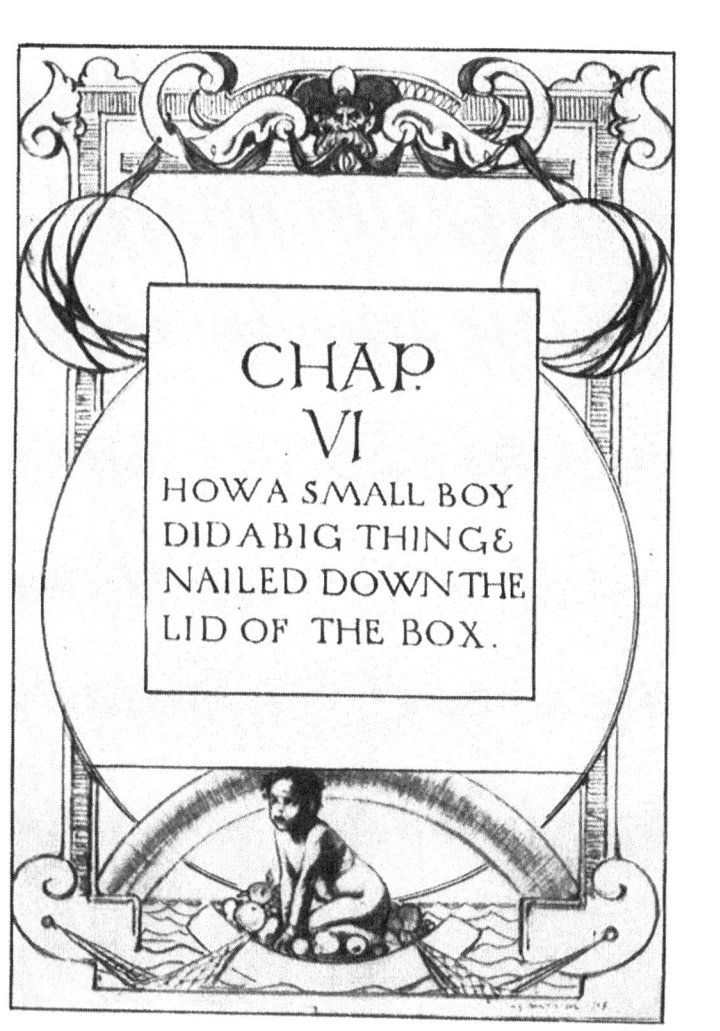

CHAP. VI

HOW A SMALL BOY
DID A BIG THING &
NAILED DOWN THE
LID OF THE BOX.

VI

NEWTON went to the pond, because he said
he was going out for that purpose, and it
might be convenient to be able to swear that
he had really been down to the water's edge.
As if to enjoy the pleasure of anticipation,
too, he had his skates with him in a green
flannel bag, though it was quite out of the
question that the ice should bear already, and
it was not even likely that the water would be
already frozen over. However, he took the
skates with him, a very good pair, of a new
model, which his father had given him towards
the end of the previous winter, so that he had
not used them more than half a dozen times.

It was very cold, but of course the ice

would not bear yet. The sun had not set, and as he was already half-way to the town, the boy apparently thought he might as well go on instead of returning at once to the cottage, where he would have to occupy himself with his books till supper-time, supposing that it occurred to his father to have any supper in his present condition. The prospect was not wildly gay, and besides, something must be done at once. Newton was possessed by that idea.

When Overholt had been alone for some time, he got up from the horsehair sofa and crept up the stairs, leaning on the shaky bannister like an old man. In his own room he plunged his face into icy cold water again and again, as if it were burning, and the sharp chill revived his nerves a little. There was no stove in the room, and before midnight the water would be frozen in the pitcher. He sat down and rubbed his forehead and wondered whether he was really any better, or was only imagining or even pretending that he was, because he wanted to be. Our own reflections about our own sensations are never so silly as at the greatest moments in our lives, because the tremendous strain on the higher faculties releases all the little ones, as in sleep, and they behave and reason as idiotically as they do in dreams, which is saying a good deal. Perhaps lunatics are only people who are perpetually asleep and dreaming with one part of their brains while the other parts are awake. They certainly behave as if that were the matter, and it seems a rational explanation of ordinary insanity, curable or incurable. Did you ever talk to a lunatic? On the subject on which he is insane he thinks and talks as you do when you are dreaming; but he may be quite awake and sensible about all other matters. He dreams he is rich, and he goes out and orders cartloads of things from shops. Pray, have you never dreamt that you were rich? Or he dreams that he is a poached egg, and must have a piece of toast to sit down upon. I believe that well-known story of a lunatic to be founded on fact. Have you never dreamt that you were somebody or something quite different from yourself? Have you never dreamt that you were an innocent man, persecuted, tried for a crime, and sentenced to prison, or even death? And yet, at the same time, in your dream, you were behaving with the utmost good sense about everything else. When you are dreaming, you are a perfect lunatic ; why may it not be true that the waking lunatic is really dreaming all the time, with one part of his brain ?

John Henry Overholt was apparently wide awake, but he had been morally stunned that day ; he was dreaming that he was going crazy, and he could not, for the life of him, tell whether he really felt any better after cooling his head in the basin than before, though it seemed immensely important to find out, just then. Afterwards, when it was all over, and things were settled again, he remembered only a blank time, which had lasted from the moment when he had broken down before the little City until he found himself sitting in the parlour alone before the supper table with a bright lamp burning, and wondering why his boy did not come home. The dream was over then ; his head ached a good deal and he did not feel hungry, but that was all ; burning anxiety had cooled to leaden care. He knew quite well that it was all over with the Motor, that his friends at the College would find him some sort of employment, and that in due time he would succeed in working off his debt to the bank, dollar by dollar. He had got his soul back out of the claws of despair that had nearly flown away with it. There was no hope, but he could live without it because he must not only live himself, but keep his boy alive. Somehow, he would get along on credit for a week or two, till he could get work. At all events there were his tools to sell, and the Motor must go for old brass, bronze, iron, and steel. He would see about selling the stuff the next day, and with what it would bring he could at least pay cash for necessaries, and the bank must wait. There was no hope in that, but there was the plain sense of an honest man. He was not a coward; he had only been brutally stunned, and now that he had recovered from the blow he would do his duty. But an innocent man who walks steadily to endure an undeserved death is not a man that hopes for anything, and it was like death to Overholt to give up his invention.

The door opened and Newton came in quietly. His face was flushed with the cold and his eyes were bright. What was the weight of leaden care to the glorious mainspring of healthy thirteen? Overholt was proud of his boy, nevertheless, for facing the dreary prospect of no Christmas so bravely. Then he had a surprise.

"I've got a little money, father. It's not much, I know, but it's something to go on with for a day or two. There it is."

Newton produced three well-worn dollar bills and some small change, which his father stared at in amazement.

"There's three dollars and seventy cents," he said. "And you told me you had four or five dollars left."

Before he sat down he piled the change neatly on the bills beside his father's plate ; then he took his seat, very red indeed and looking at the table-cloth.

"Where on earth did you get it?" asked Overholt, leaning back in his chair.

"Well"—the boy hesitated and got redder still — "I didn't steal it, anyway," he said. "It's mine all right. I mean it's yours."

"Of course you didn't steal it!" cried John Henry. "But where did you get it? You haven't had more than a few cents at a time for weeks and weeks, so you can't have saved it !"

"IT'S MINE ALL RIGHT. I MEAN ITS YOURS."

THE LITTLE CITY OF HOPE

"I didn't beg it either," Newton answered.

"Or borrow it, my boy?"

"No! I wasn't going to borrow money I couldn't pay! I'd rather not tell you, all the same, father! At least, I earned twenty cents of it. That's the odd twenty, that makes the three seventy. I don't mind telling you that."

"Oh, you earned twenty cents of it? Well, I'm glad of that, anyhow. What did you do?"

"I sort of hung round the depôt till the train came in, and I carried a man's valise across to the hotel for him. He gave me ten cents. Some of the boys do that, you know, but I thought you wouldn't care to have me do it till I had to!"

"That's all right. It does you credit. How about the other ten cents?"

"Old Bangs saw me pass his shop, and he asked me to come in and said he'd give me ten cents if I'd do some sums for him. I guess he's pretty busy just now. He said he'd give me ten cents every day till Christmas if I'd come in after school and do the sums. His boy's got mumps or something, and can't. There's no harm in that, is there, father?"

THE LITTLE CITY OF HOPE

"Harm! I'm proud of you, my boy. You'll win through—some day!"

It was the first relief from his misery the poor man had felt since he had read the letter about the overdraft in the morning.

"What I can't understand is the rest of the money," said Overholt.

Newton looked very uncomfortable again, and moved uneasily on his chair.

"Oh well, I suppose I've got to tell you," he said, looking down into his plate and very busy with his knife and fork. "Say, you won't tell mother, will you? She wouldn't like it."

"I won't tell her."

"Well"—the boy hesitated—"I sold some things," he said at last, in a low voice.

"Oh! There's no great harm in that, my boy. What did you sell?"

"My skates and my watch," said Newton, just audibly. "You see I didn't somehow feel as if I were going to skate much this winter—and I don't really need to know what time it is if I start right by the clock to go to school. I say, don't tell mother. She gave me the watch, you know, last Christmas.

82

THE LITTLE CITY OF HOPE

Of course, you gave me the skates, but you'll understand better than she would."

Overholt was profoundly touched, for he knew what delight the good skates meant in the cold weather, and the pride the boy had felt in the silver watch that kept such excellent time. But he could not think of much to say just then, for the sight of the poor little pile of dirty money that was the sordid price of so much pleasure and satisfaction half-choked him.

"You're a brave boy," he said in a low tone.

But Newton was indefinitely far from understanding that he had done anything brave; he merely felt much better now, because he had confessed and had the matter off his mind.

"Oh well, you see, something had to be done quick," he said, "and I couldn't think of anything else. But I'll go and earn that ten cents of Bangs every afternoon, you bet! And I guess I can pick up a quarter at the depôt now and then; that is, if you don't mind. It isn't much, I know, but it'll help a little."

"It's helped already, more than you have any idea," said Overholt.

83

THE LITTLE CITY OF HOPE

He remembered with bitter shame how he had completely broken down before his son that afternoon, and how quietly the lad had gone off to make his great sacrifice, pretending that he only wanted to see whether the pond was freezing.

"Well," said Newton, "I'm glad you don't think it was mean of me to go and sell the watch mother gave me. And I'm glad you feel better. You do feel a good deal better, don't you?"

"A thousand times better!" answered Overholt, almost cheerfully.

"I'm glad. Maybe you'll feel like working on the City a little after supper."

"I was afraid Hope had given us up to-day, and had flown away for good and all," said the inventor. "But you've brought her home with you again, bless you! Yes, we'll do some work after supper, and after you go to bed I'll just have one more good evening with the Motor before I give it up for ever."

Newton looked up.

"You aren't going to give it up for ever," he said in a tone of conviction. "You can't."

Overholt explained calmly enough that he

must sell the machine for old metal the very next day, and sell the tools too. But the boy shook his head.

"You'll curl up and die if you do that," he said. "Besides, if mother were here she wouldn't let you do it, so you oughtn't to. The reason why she's gone to be a governess is because she wouldn't let you give up the Motor, father. You know it is."

"Yes. It's true—but———" he hesitated.

"You simply can't do it, that's all. So I'm perfectly certain you won't! I believe everything will come round all right, anyway, if you only don't worry. That's what I believe, father."

"It's a hopeful view, at all events. The only objection to it is that it's a good deal like dreaming, and I've no right to dream any more. When you see that I'm going to, you must make me sit up and mind my lesson!"

He even laughed a little, and it was not badly done, considering that he did it on purpose to show how he meant to make the best of it all, though Hope would not do anything for him. He ate something too, if only to keep the hungry boy company.

85

THE LITTLE CITY OF HOPE

They went into the workshop, and found
the bright moonlight streaming through the
window that looked east. It fell full on the
motionless Motor, under its plate-glass case,
and turned all the steel and brass to silver and
gold, and from the clean snow that covered
the desolateness of the yard outside the moon
sent a white reflection upwards that mingled
with the direct moonlight in a ghostly sort of
way. Newton stood still and looked at the
machine, while Overholt felt about for matches.

" If only it would begin to move now, just
of itself ! "

The man knew that it would not, and
wished that the boy would not even suggest
such a thing, and he sighed as he lit the
lamp. But all the same he meant to spend
half the night in taking a last farewell of the
engine, and of all the parts on which he had
spent months and years, only to let them be
broken up for old metal in the end.

The two sat down on each side of the
little City and went to work to build the railway station ; and after all, when Overholt
looked at the Common and the College and
remembered how happy he had been there, he
began to feel that since dreams were nothing

but dreams, except that they were a great waste of time and money, and of energy and endurance, he might possibly find some happiness again in the old life, if he could only get back to it.

So Hope came back, rather bedraggled and worn out after her long excursion, and took a very humble lodging in the little City which had once been all hers and the capital of her kingdom. But she was there, all the same, peeping out of a small window to see whether she would be welcome if she went out and took a little walk in the streets.

For the blindest of all blind people are those who have quite made up their minds not to see ; and the most miserable of all the hopeless ones are those that wilfully turn their backs on Hope when she stands at the next corner holding out her hand rather timidly.

But Overholt was not one of these, and he took it gladly when it was offered, and stood ready to be led away by a new path, which was not the road to fame or wealth, but which might bring him to a quiet little place where he could live in peace with those he loved, and after all that would be a great deal.

CHAP.
VII
HOW A LITTLE WOMAN
DID A GREAT DEED
TO SAVE THE CITY.

VII

A FORTNIGHT earlier Mrs. Overholt had
been much disturbed in her mind, for she
read each of her husband's letters over at
least three times, and Newton's fortnightly
scrawls even oftener, because it was less easy
to make them out ; but she had understood
one thing very well, and that was that there
was no more money for the invention, and
very little cash for the man and the boy to
live on.   If she had known what a dreadful
mistake John Henry had made about debit
and credit, the little woman would have been
terribly anxious ; but as it was, she was quite
unhappy enough.

Overholt had written repeatedly of his

attempts to raise just a little more money with which to finish the invention, and he had explained very clearly what there was to do, and somehow she had always believed in the idea, because he had invented that beautiful scientific instrument with which his name was connected, but she was almost sure that in working out his theory he was quite on the wrong track. She did not really understand the engine at all, but she was quite certain that when a thing was going to succeed, it succeeded from the first, without many hitches or drawbacks. Most women are like that.

She had never written this to her husband, because she would do anything rather than discourage him ; but she had almost made up her mind to write him a letter of good advice at last, begging him to go back to teaching for the present, and only to work at the invention in his spare time. Just then, however, she came across a paragraph in a German newspaper in Munich which said that a great scientific man in Berlin had completed an air-motor at last, after years of study, and that it worked tolerably, enough to demonstrate the principle, but could never be of any practical use because the chemical product on which it ultimately depended was so enormously expensive.

Now Mrs. Overholt knew one thing certainly about her husband's engine, namely, that the chemical he meant to use cost next to nothing, so that if the principle were sound, the Motor would turn out to be the cheapest in existence ; and she was a practical person, like her boy Newton.

Moreover, she loved John Henry with all her heart and soul, and thought him one of the greatest geniuses in the world, and she simply could not bear the idea that he should not have a fair chance to finish the machine and try it.

Lastly, Christmas was coming ; the girls she was educating talked of nothing else, and counted the days, and sat up half the night on the edges of each other's beds discussing the beautiful presents they were sure to receive ; and a great deal might be written about what they said, but it has nothing to do with this story, except that their chatter helped to fill the air with the Christmas spirit, and with thoughts of giving as well as of receiving. Though they were rather spoiled children, they were generous too, and they laid all sorts of little traps in order to find out what their governess would like best from each of them, for they were fond of her in their way.

Also, Munich is one of the castles which King Christmas still holds in absolute sway and calls his own, and long before he is really awake after his long rest he begins to stir and laugh in his sleep, and the jolly colour creeps up and spreads over his old cheeks before he thinks of opening his eyes, much less of getting up and putting on his crown. And now that he was waking, Helen Overholt felt the old loving longing for her dear ones rising to her womanly heart, and she planned little plans for another and a happier year to come, and meanwhile she bought two or three little gifts to send to the cottage in far Connecticut.

But when she had read about the Berlin professor and his motor and thought of her own John Henry making bricks without straw and bearing up bravely against disappointment, and still writing so cheerfully and hopefully in spite of everything, she simply could not stand it another day. As I have said, King Christmas turned over just before waking, and he put out a big generous hand in his sleep and laid it on her heart. Whenever he does that to anybody, man, woman, or child, a splendid longing seizes them to give all they have to the one child, or woman, or man that each loves best, or to the being of all others that is most in need, or to help the work which seems to each of them the noblest and the best, if they are grown up and are lonely.

This is what happened to Helen Overholt, in spite of her good sense and all her practical resolutions. As long as she had anything to give, John Henry should have it and be happy, and succeed, if success were possible. She had saved most of her salary for a long time past, spending as little as she well could on herself. He should have it all, for love's sake, and because she believed in him, and because Christmas was waking up, and had laid his great affectionate old hand on her.

So it came to pass that when Overholt was pottering over the beautiful motionless Motor, late at night, sure that it would work if he had a little more money, but still more sure that it must be sold for old metal the next morning, to buy bread for the boy, even at that

hour help was near, and from the hand he
loved best in the world, which would make
it ten thousand times sweeter when it reached
him.

It was going to be an awful wrench to
give up the invention, for now, at the moment
of abandoning it, he saw, or thought he saw,
that he was right at last, and that it could
not fail. It was useless to try it as it was,
yet he would, just once more. He adjusted
the tangent-balance and the valves ; he put in
the supply of the chemical with the long name
and screwed down the hermetic plug. With
the small hand air-pump he produced the
first vacuum which was necessary ; all was
ready, every joint and stuffing-box was lubri-
cated, the spring of the balance was adjusted
to a nicety. But the engine would not start,
though he turned the fly-wheel with his hand
again and again, as if to encourage it. Of
course it would not turn alone ! He understood perfectly that the one piece on which
all depended must be made over again, exactly
the other way. That was all !

There was the wooden model of it, all
ready for the foundry that would not cast
it for nothing. If only the wooden piece

would serve for a moment's trial! But he knew that this was folly; it would not stand the enormous strain an instant, and the joints could not possibly be made air-tight.

He was utterly worn out by all he had been through during the long day, and he fell asleep in his chair towards morning, his head on his breast, his feet struck out straight before him, one arm hanging down beside him and his other hand thrust into his pocket. He looked more like a shabby lay figure stuffed with sawdust than like a living man. If Newton had come down and found him lying there under the lamplight he would have started back and shuddered, and waited a while before he could find courage to come nearer.

But the man was only very sound asleep, and he did not wake till the December dawn gleamed through the clear winter's sky and made the artificial light look dim and smoky; and when he opened his eyes it was he himself who started to find himself there in the cold before his great failure, in broad daylight.

Nevertheless, he had slept soundly, and felt better able to face all the trouble that was in store for him. He stirred the embers in the stove, put in some kindling and a supply of coal, and warmed himself, still heavy with sleep, and glad to waken consciously, by degrees, and to feel that his resolution was not going to break down.

When he felt quite himself he left the room and went upstairs cautiously, lest he should wake the boy, though it was really time to get up, and Newton was already dressing.

" I'll walk into town with you," said Overholt when they were at breakfast in the parlour. " It will do me good to get some air, and I must see about selling those things. There's no time to be lost."

Newton swallowed his hominy and bread and butter and milk, and reflected on the futility of the sacrifice he had made, since his father insisted on selling everything for old metal ; but he said nothing, because he was dreadfully disappointed.

Near the town they met the postman. As a rule Barbara got the mail when she went to market, and Overholt was not even going to ask the man if there were any letters for him. But the postman stopped him. There was one from his wife, and it was registered. He signed the little receipt for it, the man passed

" SHE'S SAVED IT ALL FOR ME, BOY. DO YOU UNDERSTAND ? "

them on his rounds, and they slackened their pace as Overholt broke the seal.

He uttered a loud exclamation when he had glanced at the contents, and he stood still in the road. Newton stared at him in surprise.

" A thousand dollars ! " he cried, overcome with amazement. " A thousand dollars ! Oh, Helen, Helen—you've saved my life ! "

He got to the side of the road and leaned against the fence, clutching the letter and the draft in his hand, and gazing into his son's face, half crazy with delight.

" She's saved it all for me, boy. Do you understand ? Your mother has saved all her salary for the Motor, and here it is ! Look at it, look at it ! It's success, it's fame, it's fortune for us all ! Oh, if she were only here ! "

Newton understood and rejoiced. He forgot his poor little attempt to help, and his own disappointment, and everything except the present glorious truth—not unadorned by the pleasant vision of the Christmas turkey, vast now, and smoking, and flanked by perfect towers of stiff cranberry jelly, ever so much better than mere liquid cranberry sauce ; in the middle distance, behind the noble dish, a noble pyramid of ice-cream raised its height, and yellow cream-cakes rose beyond, like many little suns on the far horizon. In that first moment of delight there was almost a Christmas tree, and the mother's face beside it ; but that was too much ; they faded, and the rest remained, no mean forecast of a jolly time.

"That's perfectly grand !" Newton cried when he got his breath after his surprise at the announcement. "Besides, I told you so. What did I say ? She wouldn't let you give up the Motor ! I knew she wouldn't ! Who's right now, father ? That's something like what I call a mother ! But then she always was !"

He was slightly incoherent, but that did not matter at all. Nothing mattered. In his young beatific vision he saw the bright wheel going round and round in a perfect storm of turkeys, and it was all his mother's doing.

Overholt only half heard, for he had been reading the letter ; the letter of a loving wife who believes in her husband and gives him all she has for his work, with every hope, every encouragement, and every blessing and Christmas wish.

THE LITTLE CITY OF HOPE

" There's no time to be lost ! " Overholt said, repeating the words he had spoken in a very different mood and tone half an hour earlier. " I won't walk on with you, my boy, for I must go back and get the wooden model for the foundry. They'll do it for me now, fast enough ! And I can pay what I owe at the bank, and there will be plenty left over for your Christmas too ! "

" Oh, bother my Christmas, father ! " answered Newton with a fine indifference which he did not feel. " The Motor's the thing ! I want to see that wheel go round for a Christmas present ! "

" It will ! It shall ! It must ! I promise you that ! " The man was almost beside himself with joy.

No misgiving disturbed him. He had the faith that tosses mountains aside like pebbles, now that the means were in his hand. He had the little fulcrum for his lever, which was all Archimedes required to move the world. He had in him the certainty of being right that has sent millions of men to glory or destruction.

That day was one of the happiest in all his life, either before or afterwards. He could have believed that he had fallen asleep at the moment when he had quite broken down, and that a hundred years of change had glided by, like a watch in the night, when he opened his wife's letter and wakened in a blaze of joy and hope and glorious activity. Nothing he could remember of that kind could compare with his pride and honourable satisfaction when he walked into the bank two hours afterwards, with his head high, and said he should be glad to take up the note he had signed yesterday and have the balance of the cheque placed to his credit; and few surprises which the partner who had obliged him could recollect, had equalled that worthy gentleman's amazement when the debt was paid so soon.

"If you had only told me that you would be in funds so soon, Mr. Overholt," he said, "I should not have thought of troubling you. Here is your note. Will you kindly look at it and tear it up?"

"I did not know," answered Overholt, doing as he was told.

It is a curious fact that the little note lay in a locked drawer of the partner's magnificent table, instead of being put away in the safe

with other and larger notes, where it belonged.
It may seem still stranger that, on the books,
Overholt's account showed that it had been
balanced by a deposit exactly equal to the
deficit, made by the partner himself, instead
of by crediting the amount of the note.   But
Overholt never knew this, for a pass-book
had always been a mystery to him, and made
his head ache.   The banker had thought of
his face some time after he had gone out with
his battered umbrella and his shabby shoulders
rounded as under a burden, and somehow the
Christmas spirit must have come in quietly
and touched the rich man too, though even
the stenographer did not see what happened.
For he had once been in terrible straits himself, a quarter of a century ago, and some one
had helped him just in time, and he knew
what it meant to slink out of a big bank, in
shabby clothes, his back bowed under the
heavy weight of debt and failure.

Overholt never knew; but he expressed
his warm thanks for what now seemed a small
favour, and with his wooden model of the casting, done up in brown paper, under his arm,
he went off to the foundry in Long Island.

Much careful work had been done for him

there, and the people were willing to oblige him, and promised that the piece should certainly be ready before Christmas Day, and as much earlier as possible, and should be made with the greatest exactness which the most precise machinery and the most careful work could ensure.

This being settled, Overholt returned to New York and went to two or three places in the Bowery, well known to him, where he bought certain fine tools and pieces of the most perfectly turned steel spring, and several other small objects, which he needed for the construction of the new tangent-balance he had to make for the reversed curve. Finally, he bought a silver watch like the one Newton had sold, and a new pair of skates, presents which the boy certainly deserved, and which would make a very good show at Christmas, when they were to be produced. He felt as if he had come into a large fortune.

Moreover, when he got out of the train at his own station he went into the town, and ordered beforehand the good things for the feast, though there were three weeks still, and he wanted to pay for them in advance, because he felt inside of himself that no one could be quite sure of what might happen in twenty-one days ; but the dealers flatly refused to take his money, though they told him what the things would cost. Then Overholt did almost the only prudent thing he had done in his life, for he took the necessary money and five dollars more and sealed it up in an envelope, which he put away in a safe place. The only difficulty would lie in remembering where the place was, so he told Newton about it, and the boy wrote it down on a piece of paper which he pinned up in his own room, where he could see it. There was nothing like making sure of that turkey, he thought. And I may as well say at once that in this matter, at least, no untoward accident occurred, and the money was actually there at the appointed time. What happened was something quite different, and much more unexpected, not to say extraordinary and even amazing; and in spite of all that, it will not take very long to tell.

Meanwhile, before it happened, Overholt and the boy were perfectly happy. All day long the inventor worked at the tangent-balance, till he had brought it to such perfection that it would be affected by a variation of one-tenth of one second in the aggregate speed of ten revolutions, and an increase or decrease of a tenth of a grain in the weight of the volume of the compressed air. It was so sensitive that John Henry and Newton trod cautiously on the floor of the workshop so as not to set it vibrating under the glass clock-shade, where it was kept safe from dust and dampness.

After it had been placed there to wait for the casting, the inventor took the engine to pieces and made the small changes that would be necessary before finally putting it together again, which would probably occupy two days.

Meanwhile the little City of Hope grew rapidly, and was becoming an important centre of civilisation and commerce, though it was only made of paper and chips, and bits of matchboxes and odds and ends cleverly put together with glue and painted ; except the people in the street. For it was inhabited now, and though the men and women did not move about, they looked as if they might, if they were only bigger. Overholt had seen the population in the window of a German toy-shop one day when he was in New York to get a new crocusing wheel for polishing some of the small parts of the engine. They were the smallest doll - people he had ever seen, and were packed by dozens and dozens in Nuremberg toy-boxes, and cost very little, so he bought a quantity of them. At first Newton rather resented them, just because they were only toys, but his father explained to him that models of human figures were almost necessary to models of buildings, to give an idea of the population, and that when architects make coloured sketches of projected houses, they generally draw in one or two people for that reason ; and this was perfectly satisfactory to the boy, and saved his dignity from the slight it would have suffered if he had been actually seen amusing himself with mere playthings.

Overholt was divinely happy in anticipation of the final success that was so near, and in the daily work that was making it more and more a certainty, as he thought ; and then, when the day was over, he was just as happy with the little City, which was being decorated for Christmas, with wreaths in the windows of the houses, and a great many more holly - trees than had at first been thought of, and numberless little Christmas booths round the common, like those in Avenue A, south of Tompkins Square, in New York, which make you fancy you are in Munich or Prague if you go and see them at the right hour on Christmas Eve.

Before long Overholt received a short note from the President of his old College, simply saying that the latter knew of no opening at present, but would bear him in mind. But that did not matter now.

So the two spent their time very pleasantly during the next weeks ; but though Overholt was so hopeful and delighted with his work, he knew that he was becoming nervous and overwrought by the great anticipation, and that he could not stand such a strain very long.

Then, two days before Christmas, he received a note saying that the new piece was finished and had been sent to him by express. That was almost too much happiness to bear, and when he found the heavy case at the station the next morning, and got it put on a cart, his heart was doing queer things, and he was as white as a sheet.

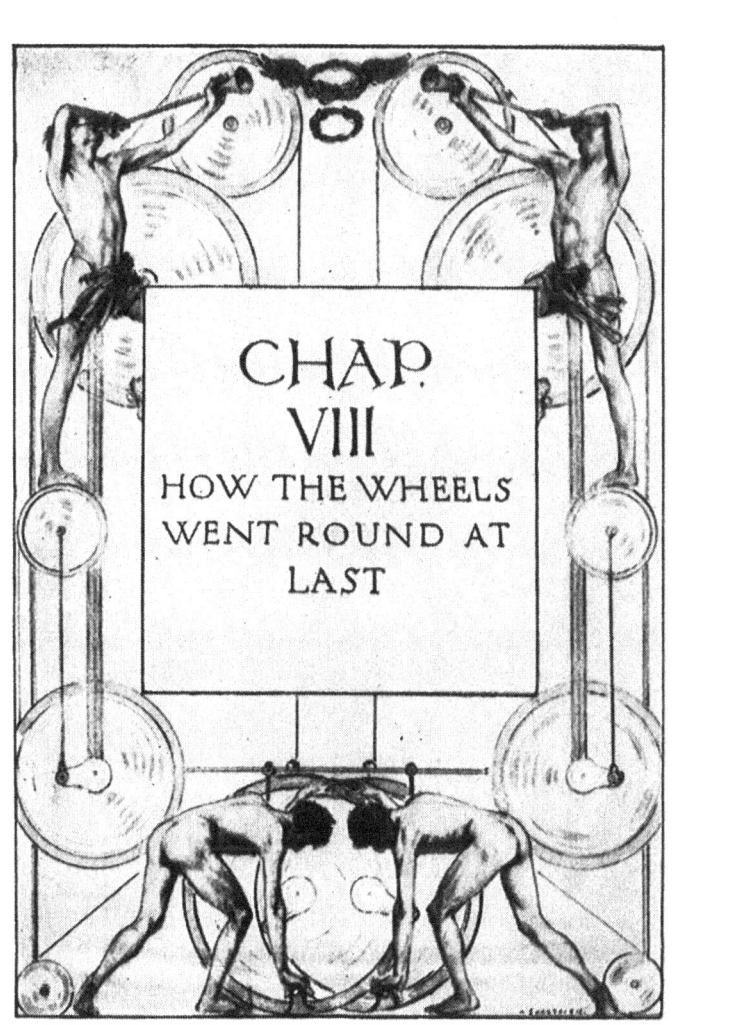

CHAP. VIII

HOW THE WHEELS WENT ROUND AT LAST

VIII

THE hush of Christmas Eve lay upon the tumble-down cottage, and on the soft fresh snow outside, and the lamps were burning quietly in the workshop, where father and son were sitting before the finished Motor.

The little City was there too, but not between them now, though Newton had taken off its brown paper cover in honour of the great event which was about to take place.

In order to be doubly sure of the result, and dreading even the possibility of a little disappointment, Overholt had decided that he would subject the only chemical substance which the machine consumed to a final form of refinement by heat, melting, boiling and cooling it, all of which would require an hour or more before it was quite ready. He felt like a man who is going to risk his life over a precipice, trusting to a single rope for safety ; that one rope must not be even a little chafed ; if possible each strand must be perfect in itself, and all the strands must be laid up without a fault. Of the rest, of the machine itself, Overholt felt absolutely sure ; yet although a slight impurity in the chemical could certainly not hinder the whole from working, it might interfere with the precision of the revolutions, or even cause the engine to stop after a few hours instead of going on indefinitely, as long as the supply of the substance produced the alternate disturbance of equilibrium which was the main principle on which the machine depended.

That sweetly prophetic evening silence, before the great feast of Good Will, does not come over everything each year, even in a lonely cottage in an abandoned farm in Connecticut, than which you cannot possibly imagine anything more silent or more remote from the noise of the world. Sometimes it rains in torrents just on that night, sometimes it blows a raging gale that twists the leafless birches and elms and hickory trees like dry grass and bends the dark firs and spruces as if they were feathers, and you can hardly be heard unless you shout, for the howling and screaming and whistling of the blast.

But now and then, once in four or five years perhaps, the feathery snow lies a foot deep, fresh-fallen, on the still country-side and in the woods; and the waxing moon sheds her large light on all, and Nature holds her breath to wait for the happy day, and tries to sleep but cannot, from sheer happiness and peace. Indoors the fire is glowing on the wide hearth, a great bed of coals that will last all night, because it is not bitter weather, but only clear and cold and still, as it should be; or if there is only a poor stove, like Overholt's, the wide door is open, and a comfortable and cheery red light shines out from within upon the battered iron plate and the wooden floor beyond; and the older people sit round it, not saying much, but thinking with their hearts rather than with their heads; but small boys and girls know that interesting things have been happening in the kitchen all the afternoon, and are rather glad that the supper was not very good, because there will be the more room for good

things to-morrow ; and the grown-ups and
the children have made up any little differences
of opinion they may have had before supper-
time, because Good Will must reign, and reign
alone, like Alexander ; so that there is nothing
at all to regret, and nothing hurts anybody
any more, and they are all happy in just wishing for King Christmas to open the door
softly and make them all great people in his
kingdom. But if it is the right sort of house,
he is already looking in through the window,
to be sure that every one is all ready for him,
and that nothing has been forgotten.

Now, although Overholt's cottage was a
miserable place for a professor who had lived
very comfortably and well in a College town,
and although the thirteen-year-old boy could
remember several pretty trees, lighted up with
coloured candles and gleaming with tinsel
and gilt apples, they both felt that this was
going to be the greatest Christmas in their
lives, because the motionless Motor was going
to move, and that would mean everything—
most of all to both of them, the end of the
mother's exile, and her speedy home-coming.
Therefore neither said anything for a long
time while the chemical stuff was slowly

warming itself and getting ready, inside a big iron pot, of which the cover was screwed on with a high-temperature thermometer sealed in it, and which stood on the top of the stove where Overholt could watch the scale.

He would really have preferred to be alone for the first trial, but it was utterly impossible to think of sending the boy to bed. He was sure of success, it is true, yet he would far rather have been left to himself till that success was no longer in the future, but present; then at last, even if Newton had been asleep, he would have waked him and brought him downstairs again to see his triumph. The lad's presence made him nervous, and suggested a failure which was all but impossible. More than once he was on the point of trying to explain this to Newton, but when he glanced at the young face he could not find it in his heart to speak. If he only asked the boy, as a kindness, to go into the next room for five minutes while the machine was being started, he knew what would happen. Newton would go quietly, without a word, and wait till he was called; but half his Christmas would be spoilt by the disappointment he would try hard to hide.

Had they not suffered together, and had not the boy sacrificed the best of his small possessions, dearly treasured, to help in their joint distress? It would be nothing short of brutal to deprive him of the first moment of triumphant surprise, that was going to mean so much hereafter. Yet the inventor would have given anything to be alone. He was overwrought by the long strain that had so often seemed unbearable, and when the liquid that was heating had reached the right temperature and the iron pot had to be taken off the stove, his hands shook so that he nearly dropped it; but Newton did not see that.

"It's wonderful how everything has come out just right!" the boy exclaimed as he looked at the machine. "Out of your three wishes you'll get two, father, for the wheel will go round and I'm going to have a regular old patent, double-barrelled Christmas with a gilt edge!" His similes were mixed, but effective in their way. "And you'll probably get the other wish in half a shake now, for mother'll come right home, won't she?"

"If the trial succeeds," Overholt said, still instinctively seeking to forestall a disappointment he did not expect. "Nothing is a fact until it has happened, you know!"

"Well," said Newton, "if I had anything to bet with, and somebody to bet against, I'd bet, that's all. But I haven't. It's a pity too, now that everything's coming out right. Do you remember how we were trying to make bricks without straw less than a month ago, father? It didn't look just then as if we were going to have a roaring old Christmas this year, did it?"

He chattered on happily, looking at the Motor all the time, and Overholt tried to smile and answered him with a word or two now and then, though he was becoming more and more nervous as the minutes passed and the supreme moment came nearer. In his own mind he was going over the simple operations he had to perform to start the engine; yet easy as they were he was afraid that he might make some fatal mistake. He did not let himself think of failure; he did not dare to wonder how he should tell his wife if anything went wrong and all her hard-saved earnings were lost in the general ruin that must follow if the thing would not move. There was next to nothing left of what she had sent, now that everything was paid for; it would support him and the boy for a month, if so long, but certainly no more.

He was ready at last, but, strange to say, he would gladly have put off the great moment for half an hour now that there was no reason for waiting another moment. He sat down again in his chair and folded his hands.

"Aren't you going to begin, father?" asked Newton. "What are you waiting for?"

Overholt pulled himself together, rose with a pale face, and laid his shaking hands on the heavy plate-glass case. It moved upwards by its chain and counterpoise, almost at a touch, till it was near the low ceiling, quite clear of the machine.

He was very slow in doing what was still necessary, and the boy watched him in breathless suspense, for he had seen other trials that had failed—more than two or three, perhaps half a dozen. Every one who has lived with an inventor, even a boy, has learned to expect disappointment as inevitable; only the seeker himself is confident up to a certain point, and then his own hand trembles, when the moment of trial is come.

Overholt poured the chemical into the chamber at the base, screwed down the air-tight plug, and opened the communication between the reservoir and the machine. Then he took out his watch and waited four minutes, that being twice the time he had ascertained to be necessary for a sufficient quantity of the liquid to penetrate into the distributors beyond. He next worked the hand air-pump, keeping his eye on the vacuum gauge, and lastly, as soon as the needle marked the greatest exhaustion he knew to be obtainable, he moved the starting lever to the proper position, and then stepped back to watch the result.

For a moment, in the joy of anticipation, a strange light illuminated his face, his lips parted as in a foretasted wonder, and he forgot even to drop the hand he had just withdrawn. The boy held his breath uncon-sciously till he was nearly dizzy.

Then a despairing cry burst from the wretched man's lips, he threw up his hands as if he had been shot through the heart, and stumbled backwards.

THE LITTLE CITY OF HOPE

The Motor stood still, motionless as ever, and gleaming under the brightly shining lamps.

"Oh, Helen! God forgive me!"

With the words he fell heavily to the floor, and lay there, a nerveless, breathless heap. Newton was kneeling beside him in an instant.

"Father!" cried the boy in agony, bending over the still white face. "Father! Speak to me! You can't be dead—you can't——"

In his mortal terror the lad held each breath till it seemed as if his head must burst, then breathed once and shut his lips again with all his strength. Some instinct made him lay his ear to the man's chest to listen for the beatings of his heart, but he could hear nothing.

Half-suffocated with sudden mingled grief and fright, he straightened himself on his knees and looked up at the cursed machine that had wrought such awful destruction.

Then he in turn uttered a cry, but it was low and full of wonder, long drawn out and trembling as the call of a frightened young wild animal.

"OH, HELEN! GOD FORGIVE ME!"

THE LITTLE CITY OF HOPE

The thing was moving, steadily, noiselessly moving in the bright light ; the double levers worked like iron jaws opening and shutting regularly, the little valve-rods rose and sank, and the heavy wheel whirled round and round. The boy was paralysed with amazement, and for ten seconds he forgot that he was kneeling beside his father's fallen body on the floor ; then he felt it against him and it was no longer quite still.

Overholt groaned and turned upon his side as his senses slowly came back and his agony tortured him to life again. Instantly the boy bent over him.

" Father ! It's going ! Wake up, father ! The wheel's going round at last ! "

CHAP.
IX
HOW THE KING OF
HEARTS MADE A
FEAST IN THE
CITY OF HOPE

IX

WHEN Overholt understood what he heard, he
opened his eyes and looked up into his son's
face, moving his head mournfully from side
to side as it lay on the boards. But suddenly
he caught sight of the engine. He gasped
for breath, his jaw dropped, and his eyes were
starting from their sockets as he struggled to
get up with the boy's help.

His voice came with a sort of rasping
scream that did not sound human, and then
broke into wild laughter, interrupted by
broken words.

"Mad!" he cried. "I knew it—it had to
come—my boy—help me to get away from that
thing—I'm raving mad—I see it moving——"

"But it really is moving, father ! Wake up ! Look at it ! The wheel is going round and round ! "

Then Overholt was silent, sitting up on the floor and leaning against his arm. Slowly he realised that he was in his senses, and that the dream of long years had come true. Not a sound broke the stillness, so perfect was the machinery, except a kind of very soft hum made by the heavy fly-wheel revolving in the air.

"Are you sure, boy ? Aren't we dreaming ?" he asked in a low tone.

"It's going like clock-work, as sure as you're born," the lad answered. "I think your falling down shook it up and started it. That was all it wanted."

The inventor got up slowly, first upon his knees, at last to his feet, never once taking his eyes from the beautiful engine. He went close to it, and put out his hand, till he felt the air thrown off by the wheel, and he gently touched the smooth, swift-turning rim with one finger, incredulous still.

"There's no doubt about it," he said at last, yielding to the evidence of touch and sight. "It works, and it works to perfection. If it doesn't stop soon, it will go on for twenty-four hours!"

Almost as much overcome by joy as he had been by despair, he let himself sink into his seat.

"Get me that tea-bottle," he said unsteadily. "Quick! I feel as if I were going to faint again!"

The draught he swallowed steadied his nerves, and then he sat a long time quite silent in his unutterable satisfaction, and Newton stood beside him watching the moving levers, the rising and sinking valve rods, and the steadily whirling wheel.

"She did it, my boy," Overholt said at last, very softly. "Your mother did it! Without her help the Motor would have been broken up for old metal three weeks ago."

"It's something like a Christmas present," Newton answered. "But then I always said she wouldn't let you give it up. Do you know, father, when you fell just now, I thought you were dead, you looked just awful! And it was quite a long time before I saw that the Motor was moving. And then, when I did see it, and thought you were dead —well, I can't tell you——"

THE LITTLE CITY OF HOPE

"Poor little chap! But it's all right now, my boy, and I haven't spoilt your Christmas, after all!"

"Not quite!"

Newton laughed joyfully, and, turning round, he saw the little City smiling on its board in the strong light, with the tiny red and green wreaths in the windows and the pretty booths, and the crowds of little people buying Christmas presents at them.

"They're going to have a pretty good time in the City too," the boy observed. "They know just as well as we do that Hope has come to stay now!"

But Overholt did not hear. Silent and rapt he sat in his old Shaker rocking-chair gazing steadily at the great success of his life, that was moving ceaselessly before his eyes, where motionless failure had sat mocking him but a few minutes ago; and as the wheel whirled steadily round and round, throwing off a little breeze like a fan, the cruel past was wafted away like a mist by a morning wind, and the bright future floated in and filled its place altogether and more also, as daylight shows the distance which was all hidden from

us by the close darkness we groped in before
it rose.

Overholt sat still, and saw, and wondered,
and little by little the wheel and the soft
vision of near happiness hypnotised him, for
his body and brain were weary beyond words
to tell, so that all at once his eyes were shut
and he was sleeping like a child, as happy in
dreamland as he had just been awake ; and
happier far, for there was a dear presence with
him now, a hand he loved lay quietly in his, and
he heard a sweet low voice that was far away.

The boy saw, and understood, for ever
since he had been very small he had been
taught that he must not wake his father, who
slept badly at all times, and little or not at all
when he was anxious. So Newton would not
disturb him now, and at once formed a brave
resolution to sit bolt upright all night, if
necessary, for fear of making any noise.
Besides, he did not feel at all sleepy. There
was the Motor to look at, and there was
Christmas to think of, and it was bright and
clear outside where the snow was like silver
under the young moon. He could look out
of the window as he sat, or at his father, or
at the beautiful moving engine, or at the

little City of Hope, all without doing more than just turning his head.

To tell the truth, it was not really a great sacrifice he was making, for if there is anything that strikes a boy of thirteen as more wildly exciting than anything else in the world, it is to sit up all night instead of going to bed like a Christian child; moreover, the workshop was warm, and his own room would be freezing cold, and he was so well used to the vile odour of the chemical stuff, that he did not notice it at all. It was even said to be healthy to breathe the fumes of it, as the air of a tannery is good for the lungs, or even London coal smoke.

But it is one thing to resolve to keep awake, even with many delightful things to think about; it is quite another to keep one's eyes open when they are quite sure that they ought to be shut, and that you ought to be tucked up in bed. The boy found it so, and in less than half an hour his arm had got across the back of the chair, his cheek was resting on it quite comfortably, and he was in dreamland with his father, and quite as perfectly happy.

So the two slept in their chairs under the

big bright lamps ; and while they rested the Air-Motor worked silently, hour after hour, and the heavy wheel whirled steadily on its axle, and only its soft and drowsy humming was heard in the still air.

That was the most refreshing sleep Overholt remembered for a long time. When he stirred at last and opened his eyes, he did not even know that he had slept, and forgot that he had closed his eyes when he saw the engine moving. He thought it was still nine o'clock in the evening, and that the boy might as well finish his little nap where he was, before going to bed. Newton might sleep till ten o'clock if he liked.

The lamps burned steadily, for they held enough oil to last sixteen hours when the winter darkness is longest, and they had not been lighted till after supper.

But all at once Overholt was aware of a little change in the colour of things, and he slowly rubbed his eyes and looked about him, and towards the window. The moon had set long ago ; there was a grey light on the snow outside and in the clear air, and Overholt knew that it was the dawn. He looked at his watch then, and it was nearly seven o'clock ; for in New York and Connecticut, as you may see by your pocket calendar, the sun rises at twenty-three minutes past seven on Christmas morning.

He sprang to his feet in astonishment, and at the sound Newton awoke and looked up in blank and sleepy surprise.

" Merry Christmas, my boy ! " cried Overholt, and he laughed happily.

" Not yet," answered Newton in a disappointed tone, and rubbing his arm, which was stiff. " I've got to go to bed first, I suppose."

" Oh no ! You and I have slept in our chairs all night and the sun is rising, so it's merry Christmas in earnest ! And the Motor is running still, after nine or ten hours. What a sleep we've had ! "

The boy looked out of the window stupidly, and vaguely wished that his father would not make fun of him. Then he saw the dawn, and jumped up in wild delight.

" Hurrah ! " he shouted. " Merry Christmas ! Hurrah ! hurrah ! " If anything could make that morning happier than it had promised to be, it was to have actually cheated bed for the first time in his life.

They were gloriously happy, as people

126

have a right to be, and should be, when they have been living in all sorts of trouble, with a great purpose before them, and have won through and got all they hoped for, if not quite all they could have wished—because there is absolutely no limit to wishing if you let it go on.

The people watched them curiously in church, for they looked so happy ; and for a long time the man's expression had always been anxious, if it had no longer been sad of late, and the boy's young face had been preternaturally grave ; yet every one saw that neither of them even had a new coat for Christmas Day, and that both needed one pretty badly. But no one thought the worse of them for that, and in the generous Good Will that was everywhere that morning everybody was glad to see that every one else looked happy.

In due time the two got home again ; the Motor was still working to perfection, as if nothing could ever stop it again, and Overholt oiled the bearings carefully, passed a leather over the fixed parts, and examined the whole machine minutely before sitting down to the feast, while Newton stood beside him, looking on and hoping that he would not be long.

The boy had his new watch in his pocket, and it told him that it was time for that turkey at last, and his new skates were in the parlour, and there was splendid ice on the pond where the boys had cleared away the snow, and it was the most perfect Christmas weather that ever was; and in order to enjoy everything it would be necessary to get to work soon.

The two were before the Air-Motor, turning their backs to the door; and they heard it open quietly, for old Barbara always came to call Overholt to his meals, because he was very apt to forget them.

"We are just coming," he said, without turning round. But the boy turned, for he was hungry for the good things; and suddenly a perfect yell of joy rent the air, and he dashed forward as Overholt turned sharp round.

"Mother!"

"Helen!"

And there she was, instead of in Munich. For the rich people she was with had happily smashed their automobile without hurting

'' MOTHER ! ''
'' HELEN ! ''

themselves, and had taken a fancy to spend Christmas at home ; and, after the manner of very rich people, they had managed everything in a moment, had picked up their children and the governess, had just caught the fastest steamer afloat at Cherbourg, and had arrived in New York late on Christmas Eve. And Helen Overholt had taken the earliest train that she could manage to get ready for, and had come out directly to surprise her two in their lonely cottage.

So John Henry Overholt had his three wishes after all on Christmas Day. And everybody had helped to bring it all about, even Mr. Burnside, who had said that Hope was cheap and that there was plenty of it to be had.

But as for the little Christmas City in which Hope had dwelt and waited so long, they all three put the last touches to it together, and carried it with them when they went back to the College town, where they felt that they would be happier than anywhere else in the world, even if they were to grow very rich, which seems quite likely now.

That is how it all happened.

Printed by R. & R. CLARK, LIMITED, *Edinburgh.*